The 202

2020 Annual

Written by the Elizabeth River Writers

Presented by

Stella Samuel & Dr. Charles Cooper III

2020 Annual
By the Elizabeth River Writers

Print Edition

Copyright © 2020

Cover Design by Jonas Mayes-Steger of Fantasy and Coffee Design
https://fantasyandcoffee.com/

Catalog in Publication Data Held by the Library of Congress

ISBN: 978-1-7342330-9-4

ELIZABETH RIVER
PRESS

STELLA SAMUEL

ARZONO
PUBLISHING

DEDICATION

Stella Samuel

I dedicate this project to a friendship started years ago over many miles, songs, and words, then fostered in aggravation and dedication. Also, as with every project, this is dedicated to the endless support and love of a good woman. Jessica, I cannot do this life thing without you.

Finally, to the writers who submitted, especially the writers we chose to feature who trusted us with their work, this is your place to shine. Stand up and dance! Welcome to the tribe.

Charles Cooper

I dedicate this book to my children who prove themselves to be a better version of me every day. Especially for my son who is graduating this year and leaving the comfort of home to embark upon life's grand journey.

To all those authors who refuse to put down their pen despite countless rejections and hardships, under threat of jail or death carry on, thought is freedom.

CONTENTS

FOREWORD

A foreword for Elizabeth River Press' first Annual Anthology…

This foreword needs to be momentous. It should be as momentous as the work that went into the stories and poetry contained within. It needs to be a celebration of the people to whom the work belongs. It must be a reflection of the passion with which Stella Samuel attacks everything. Make no mistake, this is a partnership, but she is the driving force behind it. Moreover, it needs to be a reflection of the purpose for which I created Elizabeth River Press. In short, this should be better than anything I've ever written, erudite, instructional, imaginative, inspirational, and momentous. With this in mind, here is a little about how this book came into being.

In the movie, *Wonder Boys*, pulled from the Michael Chabon novel of the same name, Rip Torn plays a character named Quinten, known as Q. He, a published author on the scale of Stephen King or Michael Connelly, famously introduces his speech at Word Fest by saying, "I am a writer." The phrase is hyperbole in the story and only there to give rise to laughter from the character James, a "real" writer with a gift for the craft. The moment I first heard that line, sometime around October 2000, I was asking myself a real, similar, serious question. I was an US Army soldier who wrote a lot of poetry. Soon to leave the Army, I had to answer the question, "What did I want to be since I had grown up?" The answer was obvious to me. I wanted to be a writer. What I recognized in the scene of that movie is that there are any number of types of writers. There is the professor, who has a complete understanding of the craft, who also happens to be a stoner. There is the pompous best seller who uses formulas to release the same book over and over with a different title. There is the gifted, young loner who is able to crank out a book in two weeks, a meaningful story or assignment overnight. but he is depressed, lonely, and misunderstood.

Who did I want to be? Rich would be nice, but I've never been a formula guy, and I really don't like to do the same things over and over. I don't think I'm the gifted guy because my brain runs in too many directions to capture the ideas necessary to pull that off. Depressed, lonely, and misunderstood, I have and or had a lock on those traits. At the time, I was neck deep into transcendentalism considering myself a disciple of Ralph Waldo Emerson. I wanted to know everything, reflect, and ruminate on it, and most of all, I wanted other people in the world to see what I saw. I pushed everything else to the side, and I asked myself, what does it take to not just write, but also to create something which people will read.

By the time I figured all this out, 9/11 happened, my first child was on the way, and I had a serious 50+ hour a week job working for a defense contractor. The dream to be a writer refused to die of responsibility. Instead, I used the responsibility to augment the dream. I took money from the new gig and self-published a book of poetry called, *Desperate Times*. It had the expected sales margin of a book no one knows exists, by someone no one knows is a writer. Maybe a dozen copies sold.

My important job still met all the requirements which duty levied on me. I contributed to my country. I provided for my family. The undercurrent of the dream still ran through me, though, like a haunting echo of the potential, *I could have been*. Those words still echoed in my id, "I am a writer." With all the ambition in the world, I started writing a book which took everything I had ever read and loved about government, society, and science fiction and turned it into a satirical jaunt into a dystopian future. Keep in mind that all this time, I continued to write poetry, and I found a tribe in Myspace, the social networking precursor to Facebook. On Myspace, there are thousands of poets, all posting daily or nearly daily. They read my poetry and I read theirs. We gave each other kudos and lauded the glories of the truths we found. None of this led to my poetry book selling or making a name for myself beyond this tribe.

In 2007, I finished the *Riddle of Common Sense* with the full and certain belief it was a masterpiece. It made me laugh. Certainly, if it fell in the right hands today, I could continue to add to the stack of rejection letters I received from publishers, agents, magazines, and so on. I didn't understand the grading scale these polished professionals used to grade who or what would be the next big thing in writing, and the truth is, I still don't. Seventy-eight rejection letters later, I realized I needed a different path. I dove neck deep into the online world, which was only then coming into its maturity.

I found an online company called Publish America, who would do all the publishing work for independent authors including editing, cover design, etc. in return for the names, addresses, and emails of the author's closest relatives and friends, who I am certain received a barrage of emails informing them of the book and the exorbitant price they were asking for it. There was no marketing support to speak of; however, it wasn't a vanity press. I thought, *this is a step in the right direction.*

I published the *Riddle of Common Sense* through Publish America, and immediately and forever, I regret the decision. When the edited copy came back, I found several obvious typographic errors and large sections of the book missing. The editing software they employed cut around forty thousand words. The rhythm of the text was completely dismantled, and half of the story was gone. I lived through my deal with them, contract in place. I gave them their pound of flesh. I made up my mind then and there, not to live through such an experience again. See, what I realized from my experience with Publish America and my 78 brushes with the publishing industry is this, "there is nothing they are doing, which I cannot do, and I can probably do it better."

I started work that day on forming Elizabeth River Press, with the foundational principle being, if it deserved to be in print, ERP would do everything we could to see that it happened. That was over twelve years ago. Since then, we have published more than twenty books by three authors. Why not more? Why not an exact number? Well, some of them were published as simply online books, essentially PDF documents for download. I don't know how to count them. I still have that full-time job that takes care of the family. I still read everything I get my hands on, though not as fast as I once did. I have continued to pursue other means of improving myself and my situation, but the dream remains. I still want to see my ideas and stories in people's hands and minds. I still want to be read.

I spend way too much time on Facebook with a substantial number of "friends" who have proven as least 17 times that they are not going to spend money to own a book when they can get my drivel for free online. Still, Facebook has brought connections to a lot of folks I thought were lost to memory. One of those special people is my friend Stella Samuel. Stella is an incredible woman who comes at everything with the passion and vigor of five people. I first met her in 6th grade. I don't think we talked much then. I'm fairly certain I was scared of women in general, and she was attractive enough to be intimidating. I left that school after my 7th grade year and never thought to see her again.

Skip forward six years or so, I found myself in the world of summer and Christmas employment while I was home from college. I took a job at a music store from a lady named Tracey. She introduced me to the Assistant Manager who may be nearly as anal about alphabetical order as I was, and you guessed it, she was Stella!

I joined the Army which suspended my love of music temporarily, and again, I lost touch with Stella. This time, roughly two decades would pass before we were reunited on Facebook where I was asking the question, how can I be read, and Stella was pursuing a degree in fine arts from Full Sail University. She proceeded to remind me that I had created Elizabeth River Press for writers, not just for me, and there were a lot of writers out there who are quite worthy of having their work in print who were still being tortured by publishing company executives. Two years and hundreds of hours later, Stella and I are pleased to bring you this book, including the writing of thirty-four amazing authors who will henceforth, and forever be, Elizabeth River Writers.

The 2020 Elizabeth River Writers are:

Andrew Leake

Anissa Sboui

Arianna Sebo

Bobbi Sinha-Morey

Bruce McRae

C. Marry Hultman

Camille Ziegenhagen

Christine Hennebury

Danny Barbare

DC Diamondopolous

Don Noel

Edward Lee

Eduard Schmidt-Zorner

Gerard Sarnat

James Sanchez

Jay Waitkus

Kasisi Harris

Kira Metcalf

Luisa Kay Reyes

Melissa St. Pierre

Molly Neely

Patricia Walsh

Ron Torrence

Sandy Stuckless

Shelby Wilson

Sima Greenfield

Tammera L Cooper

Tammy L. Breitweiser

Val Muller

Stella Samuel

Tammy Bird

Charles Cooper IV

THE 2020 ANNUAL

ANDREW LEAKE

Biography

My name is Andrew Leake, and I live in a small town in the East of England by the sea where it is often cold and hardly warm. I write to see if people can relate. I would say that my style is unique, and I am always on the lookout for things to do and to develop my skillset. I'm a great guy once you get to know me, and I am a terrific dancer.

Andrew Leake

One Summer

It was a wet summer
I had my socks on the whole time and I don't know why
When I roamed the fields of grey
I knew that deep down there would be hell to pay
I think I better scurry off as there is hell to pay
For those beneath the ground who fail to keep it warm
I've been thinking lately
I've been wandering aimlessly
I think I'm lost at this moment
I've committed no crime
I roam free on this land of green
And I wonder why it's so hard to see
The amount of bees that pollinate our ears.
Buzz buzz whizz whizz there's hardly a noise to be made
A maid appears and we make love on the kitchen floor
I think it's time I got out into the real world.

MOLLY NEELY

Biography

Molly Neely is an avid reader of everything from history, theology, and politics, to vampires, ghosts, and romance. Her debut novel, *The Sand Dweller*, was published by Black Opal Books in 2016. She has an eclectic style and a wide range of tastes, including a passion for Pre-Code classic movies, pretty much anything with bacon in it, and of course preparing for the Zombie apocalypse. She lives in the heart of the San Joaquin Valley, Fresno California, with her husband, Lyle, and their Whippet, Devo.

She can be found on Facebook @mollyneelywriter or on twitter @mollyneely.

There's Value In Vigilance

We've never really talked about it.

I used to do that thing we spouses all do, when they first come home.

"What's the matter?" I'd ask.

"Nothing," was his only reply.

It wasn't long before I stopped asking.

As days of celebration turned into weeks of adjustment, it was obvious there was more than 'nothing' going on. Even though my partner, the better half of myself had returned to me from a war torn country, it was clear a part of him had been left behind in the desert. His habits had changed. His tastes, his temper. I wouldn't call him broken... more like a teacup with a chip in its handle. Just harder to hold onto than it used to be.

The first change was his bedtime habits. He cries in his sleep. All the time. Sometimes it'll creep in like a low whimper. Other times the sobbing shakes the house like thunder. I imagine war planes streaking the skies in his dreams, dropping their bombs and riddling the landscape of his subconscious with invisible scars.

He mumbles too. Names. Ranks. Commands. I hear his strong voice and the men in his unit rage against the enemy. Fighting the same war night after night, his brothers in arms dying night after night. I don't know who they were. I don't know what happened to them. I just know they're gone. I know they mattered more than life and now they haunt his dreams.

I feel helpless in those moments. Afraid to wake him up, yet nervous about letting him sleep. I wonder, would I be rescuing him, or would I only make it worse? I don't know, so I do nothing. If only I could climb inside his head and see what he sees, feel what he feels. There's nothing I'd rather do, than share his burden.

His legs twitch and jerk. Like an animal fleeing danger. When he's on the move, there's no crying, only fear and adrenaline and regret. He shouts. Curses. Kicks. Constantly running headlong into a long gone danger. It frightens me. It feels like he's been deployed inside his mind.

Of course, sometimes he can't sleep at all. Sitting in the dark, his hands clasped and dangling between his legs. He stares into an invisible abyss with defeated eyes and an angry brow. There behind the blank facade, brews a hyper-vigilance. His warrior's ear, in tune to every creak and groan our home makes, captures every sound. He tries to ignore them. But eventually, the noises win, sending him down the hall to do a room by room sweep of the house.

There's something inside him, trying to crowd him out. Something that came back with him from the war. It knows if he speaks its name, if he ever shines a light on the thing that steals his will, its power over him will start to die. For light always conquers darkness. I find myself hanging by a thread, watching, waiting for him to take a breath. Listening for the name of the beast.

I want to make it all stop. I want to let loose a battle cry of my own, draw my weapon and vanquish his phantom enemies. Enemies like the nervous sweats. The sudden bolting from the bed at 2 AM. The lost look in his face and the nights full of demons only he can see. If only I could calm that pacing and racing heart that keeps him from my arms.

In the daylight, he's become a recluse. Hiding behind drawn curtains and a locked front door, trying to turn the tide of battle with the occasional regimen of pills or booze. Content to bury himself in the blue glow of a TV screen, while life and second chances pass by. The silence fills our house like fog, choking us both.

I try to be helpful, but it never seems to work out and more often than not, I just end up smothering him like a mother hen. He's right when he says I don't understand. I wasn't there for the whizzing bullets, the cries of the dying and the endless droves of faceless enemy combatants. I don't know what it's like to be hunted. To be distrustful of children. But he's wrong if he thinks I don't want to. So, for now, I hang back. Hopeful, open, and patient.

There's value in vigilance.

Then there are times when I see a spark, a fleeting glance of the man I sent off to war so long ago. He's there in a comment, a touch, a joke only he could think was funny. His former self peeks out like a groundhog in the spring. And for as long as it lasts, there's joy. He laughs and loves. He does and says all of those things that made me fall in love with him, and I do everything I can to make it last.

As they say, the struggle is real and the reality is, he's just not ready to fight his demons. Maybe he doesn't think he's strong enough to face them, or maybe he doesn't know the demons are there. Perhaps like other soldiers, he believes if he shoves them down far enough, they will disappear. That the monsters will suffocate under the weight of his resolve. I suppose there are other wives who would have abandoned this ship long ago.

But I'm not other wives.

For me, there's no retreat and no surrender. After all, he fought for me. He stood between the enemy and our way of life. So here I stand in return. A candle in the window. I'm happy to show him that no matter how long it takes, I will always be here. When the time comes, he'll call for reinforcements and then I'll be there. I'll brandish my weapon, the one I've kept clean and sharp. His demons will see that he is not the only deadly warrior in this fight.

ANISSA SBOUI

Biography

Anissa Sboui is a university professor from Sousse, Tunisia. She earned a PhD is American literature and is the author of three volumes, *Rebirth* (2018), *Transcend* (2019) and *Number One* (2020). She is married to Adel Ben Mohamed, and we have two daughters.

Anissa Sboui

August 17ᵗʰ

Green Street, Mayfair
Scorching weather
Serious affair,
Opting for silky maxi dress,
Abandoning leather.

The pregnant Lady
With red Zōri,
And a coolie hat
But!
Strong labour pains startled her…
Giving birth to a girl
Seemed a genuine matter
Not a word did she utter,
Recalling pre-Islamic barbaric fight
She read about and had deep insight
"When the female infant, buried alive, is questioned
For what crime she was killed"
It was wrong horrible deed, not right.

Ready for the nesting instinct,
Her fateful mission was
Possible as Ian Fleming might detect,
For family Bond she has longed
Her body replaced her body,
Despite fake laughter,
Mood swings,
Style to alter
Many other things:
Chloasma,
Hyperpigmentation,
Hemorrhoids,
Medical terms she wanted to shutter.

Here in the hospital

Anissa Sboui

Her womb beats her to the delivery room,
Cries do hover
Over and over.
Never cry, the mother says,
Ahead of time to cry,
You will have to adapt,
To think twice before you act,
To live or die,
To love or hate
To abide by your bitter fate,
To leave or stay,
To wipe your tears away,
Wait until you grow,
Life will obviously show,
Decades of immense triumph,
Coupled with decades of decay…

VAL MULLER

Biography

Val Muller is the author of several novels, including the *Corgi Capers Series*. After a four-year lull in her writing career due to having children, she is back in the game and writing again. Val can be found at www.valmuller.com.

Angel In The Pod

A vermillion blaze cut the darkness, night's last stronghold against dawn. The sun rose higher, from a saturated gradient of wonder to an ordinary blush of yellow against blue. The lighting shift jarred Ava out of her reverie and made her painfully aware of the mundane realities around her. The red light. The clock mocking her on the dashboard. The Morning Struggle.

7:07. Now 7:08. She was usually at work by now, catching up from the day before or planning for the day ahead. But it had been one of those mornings. The dog tore open a box of cereal while Ava was out in the garden. Then Sammy put his shoes on the wrong feet, a cup of juice got spilled on the dog, and Jenny forgot her water bottle.

Ava's phone beeped, and she flipped open her email app. A freelance client was asking about designing a logo for his custom cake business. It was a fun job, but logos always took more time than anticipated. It was difficult to brand someone, and usually it was even more difficult for business owners to accept their branding. But the client needed the logo soon and wanted to know when the drafts would be ready.

Urgh. I need more time in the day. Or if I could just function without sleep…

As she flew through a yellow light down the road, she wondered when in the world she would ever catch up. With laundry. With cleaning. With her marriage. And Sammy. Hadn't Jenny been able to read by the time she was Sammy's age? Sammy had no interest. Ava had been a better mother to Jenny. Read to her all the time. Sang alphabet songs and whatnot.

Then again, Jenny had always slept through the night.

Ahead of her, traffic slowed. There was something on the side of the road. Ava slowed too and noticed an old man standing by an ancient truck. It looked like it had a flat. Why was no one helping him? Poor guy. It was starting to drizzle.

No, you have work to catch up on, she scolded. *Just keep driving.*

She slowed long enough to see his face. He seemed to look at her particularly. His wrinkled neck peeked out of his field coat, reminding her of a wise old turtle. Slow and confident. His face was timeless. He could have stepped out of a photo from the Dustbowl era. Or a Renaissance masterpiece. His eyes seemed to know she would pull over before she did.

Her hands and feet worked without her permission, and in an instant, she was on the side of the road, her flashers on. She pulled on her jacket and hurried to the man.

"Have a flat?" She shivered in the light drizzle. Cars kept moving around her, people off to their jobs and morning commutes.

The old man nodded. "You're the first person stopped to help," he said, his voice whispery, aged, but strong underneath.

"I'm not a mechanic, but—"

"You know how to change a tire."

His eyes already knew the answer. She nodded. "My dad made me rotate all four tires by hand before he'd let me get my license."

The old man nodded. "I thought so. You're a Renaissance man. Woman, I mean."

Ava raised an eyebrow. "I can change a tire."

He scratched the back of his neck.

"Least, I could. Back in the day. Now with my knees, I get down there to change the tire, no getting back up again."

It was already 7:16.

He averted his eyes. "You look busy. You can go, you know. Someone else will stop for me."

She bit her lip. *In for a penny, in for a pound.* "I got this," she said, taking the tire iron from his trunk.

At 7:32, the tire was fixed, the old one tucked in the man's trunk. Her workpants were soiled now, two streaks of grease running down one of the legs.

"I'm sorry about that."

She shrugged. "It'll make an interesting story at work." She bit her lip. *Luckily, there are no client meetings today.*

The man reached for his wallet. "Here, let me pay you." His wallet had a few singles in it, some lint.

Ava shook her head. "It's okay." She glanced at her watch again.

The old man's face stretched into a smile. "It's time, then."

"Time?"

"It's not money. It's time. That's what you hoped I had in my wallet."

Sure, old man. "Yes. Time. That's always what I need." She forced a laugh. "Don't we all?"

"A Renaissance woman will always need time. A lifetime is not enough to do all she might accomplish." The old man kept his smile and reached deep into the wallet. "I was saving these. Here."

As if in a trance, Ava held out her palm, and the man placed two seeds into them. They were about as large as green bean seeds, but twisted and darker.

"What are they?"

"You have a garden. Plant them. Together."

Ava thought about her garden, the way it caught the sunlight on dew-covered mornings, the way everything seemed so serene and unhurried in the garden, the way the beans and pumpkins reached up with curly tendrils, their vines fibered and ribbed, the colors changing with the seasons and time of day. The way bright red tomatoes popped against greenery, the way a darkened cucumber contrasted the stark green of the lawn. The way a deep green pumpkin turning orange signaled the start of fall.

What would these seeds grow into? She had never seen them before. When she looked up to inquire, the man and his truck were gone. Ava stood alone on the side of the road, the steady stream of traffic winding around her. Then she stuck the seeds in her pocket, got in her car, and drove to work.

After work, she hurried to get the kids to their dental checkup. The dentist was running late, as always, and of course both kids had meltdowns. She had no patience left for anything by the time they left, and she picked up fast food on the way home. The dog's fur was matted and sticky from the juice incident earlier, so she bathed the kids and then the dog while her husband tucked them into bed.

A pile of dishes waited from breakfast and packed lunches, so she tackled those while Mark folded what was in the dryer. Then he opened the mail while she packed lunches for the morning.

"I'll put these away," Mark said, carrying two baskets of folded laundry.

"Thanks." She offered a smile. Mark smiled back. She was sure the dark circles under her eyes were darker than Mark's, but even he looked tired. The thought of warm bed called to her, but Benny, still damp, whined. So on with the boots and the leash. "Just to the road and back," she promised. She didn't like letting him out at night. There were foxes and skunks and sometimes bears, and Benny was known to launch after deer.

The drizzle had turned to a steadier mist, so she pulled on her jacket and grabbed the leash. Benny hurried to the end of the drive, and she stopped to let him sniff. She looked up at the way the moon illuminated a cloud to the west. It would be a beautiful photo with the backlighting, eerie and surreal, if she had the proper equipment to capture shots in the dark. But she had only her phone. It would do no justice to the beauty of the moment.

It would make an even better painting.

The thought seemed not her own, though it echoed in her head. She shivered and pulled Benny back to the house. Hand in pocket, she felt those two beans. She'd nearly forgotten about the incident this morning with the old man. In fact, everyone at work had been so busy, no one even noticed the grease stain on her pants.

She looked down at Benny, who sat, waiting expectantly. "What do you think, boy? Should we plant them?"

Benny whined, and she led him to the garden. He was not allowed inside—her plants were too delicate for his bumbling curiosity, so she hung his leash on the gate and ordered him to stay. She turned on her phone screen to illuminate the rows of tomato, cucumber, beans. In the nascent spring, they were small but burgeoning. There was a space in the corner, one she left empty in case Jenny wanted to join her in the garden. It was a place Jenny could dig without disrupting the rest of the plants.

But Jenny had been sleeping through Ava's early morning trysts in the garden, so maybe that empty patch of dirt was unnecessary. Ava put away her phone and dug with bare hand, scooping the wet earth until the hole was a few inches deep. She placed the seeds inside, one next to the other, and covered them gently, tucking them in like children. "We'll see what you are," she said, smiling.

When she got inside to shower, Mark was already asleep.

Jenny woke early the next morning, and Ava forgot about the seeds. The morning was filled with a fight over what shoes to wear and a toddler who wouldn't eat his breakfast. It wasn't until a day later that Ava went out again with Benny in the early morning to find the seeds had sprouted. They sprouted quickly, like a weed or a mushroom. She didn't recognize the plant, though its long, thick stem and large, almond-shaped pod reminded her of milkweed. Two days old and a foot tall already.

"Milkweed doesn't grow that quickly," she said, shrugging.

The seeds had each sprouted into a stem, and the two stems twisted around each other, one light green and the other darker, almost brown. The pod was large, and there was only one. She couldn't tell which of the entwined stems it grew from, and though she didn't touch it, the pod looked spongy and was covered in small excrescences that looked hard and rough, like barnacles.

Maybe the old man was crazy. Were those seeds weeds that would take over her garden? Where had he gotten them? Her mind flashed with possibilities. Could it be an invasive plant? Was she dooming her entire landscape?

She offered the tomatoes an apologetic glance before hurrying off to work.

On Saturday, Mark watched morning cartoons with the kids while Ava walked Benny. The pod had grown exponentially in size. Ava's gut told her to pull it, to chop it to bits, or even to burn it. But she couldn't. The morning sun streaming onto the pod made it sparkle. She'd never seen anything like it before. The small excrescences were now larger, shiny, almost like seashells.

When she went inside, the kids were bored. She promised to paint with Jenny while Mark took Sammy to the park. It was too chilly to paint outside, but Ava glanced toward the garden. She was relieved, actually. Something in her gut told her not to show Jenny that strange plant that seemed to be even taller this morning than the night before. Jenny painted rainbows and teddy bears, and Ava painted the pod. She used dark blues and greens, and there was something frightening about it. When Jenny saw it, she cried, then covered the whole thing in smudges of black. Ava wrinkled it into a ball and threw it in the trash.

The following Saturday, Ava rose early. The day was packed: Jenny had a friend's birthday party at ten, and Sammy had a playdate at the park a half hour after. Ava was in charge of both, since the family had procrastinated: Mark would be spending the weekend doing taxes.

Ava had woken just after four, unable to sleep. Her head spun with the endless list of tasks. The house was a mess, so she snuck downstairs to tackle the disaster of a kitchen. Dishes, counter, fridge: a marathon session left her tired and famished, and the sun was just rising. She fed Benny and let him outside. She donned a light jacket and pocketed her folding knife and spool of twine, just in case any of the garden plants needed staking already. After all, that pod had grown preternaturally quickly. Maybe the unusually warm weather would mean an early crop.

Benny left two trails of dark in the dew-drenched grass, and Ava found him circling the garden. She called him over, leashed him. The sun streaming through the dew-kissed spider webs made her want to paint—what a study in light this view would be!—so that she almost missed the woman.

When Ava saw her, she startled. Pulse raced. Stumbled backward. Who the hell was in her garden?

"Hello?" Ava called. Whispered, more like.

The woman did not respond. She sat there in the garden. Knelt, rather, in the spot usually reserved for Jenny, the one now taken by the strange pod plant. Only, the pod had now opened. Whatever noxious seeds it contained had now been expelled into the world. The pod hung empty and limp. But now this woman, in her garden…

Should she call the police? What if this was a mental patient? Someone with disabilities? A missing person? What if someone were looking for her?

"Hello? Excuse me," Ava said, louder this time.

The woman rose slowly, then turned around. Ava's palms went limp. She dropped Benny's leash. The woman was her mirror image, right down to freckles and moles. What was even happening?

Ava rose her hand to wave, and the woman waved back. Benny looked from one to the other, and although he seemed excited for the extra company, he was not acting alarmed, and he didn't bark. Then Ava laughed. She opened the gate and released the woman, patting her firmly on the back, still laughing. "Here I thought I'd been awake, but I'm only dreaming! What a strange dream," she told the woman. "It makes sense, though. Like I would really get up at four a.m. to clean the kitchen!" Her laughter rose in pitch. "I mean, that would be more like a dream come true than a nightmare, right? Having a clean kitchen?" Hysterics. "Hey, twin pod lady, come join me for tea! We can have a Mad Hatter tea party until I wake up. Benny will serve the sugar!" She giggled like a girl. Everything was funny. She dropped into the garden, the wet soil staining her clothes and coat.

The woman nodded and stepped over Ava, moving toward the house. Ava stopped laughing and followed her inside.

The kitchen was immaculate, just as she'd left it. Ava chuckled again and grabbed two coffee mugs. Then she thought better of it. She chose Jenny's two unicorn mugs, the ones Grammy had given for Christmas. A rainbow mane created the handle, and the misplaced unicorn horn posed a hazard to all who drank. Still, what better choice for a Mad Tea Party?

The woman was already heating a kettle on the stove, and Ava studied her face as the water heated. The features were exquisite, right down to the fine lines and blotches of fatigue under the eyes.

"I didn't know I had such an imagination," she told the woman. "I didn't know I knew my face so well." Then she squinted. "I didn't know I'd grown so old."

She set the mugs on the counter. The woman only stood.

"This is a strange dream. Aren't you supposed to do something symbolic? Tell me something about my life? My subconscious? Turn into a flaming bush? Warn me about a project at work or an impending illness?"

The woman only stood.

"What about this?" Ava took one of the mugs, rose it high in the air, and dropped it on the floor. It shattered spectacularly. She laughed, then turned to the woman. "Okay, dream-pod-twin. In a dream, it would probably be you who cleaned that up."

The woman knelt and began to pick up the shards just as Mark descended the stairs, yawning.

"What in god's name is going on down here? What fell?" he asked.

"Nothing," Ava said. At her feet, the woman froze. Mark could not see her from the stairs, as the kitchen's island blocked his view.

Mark looked real. Acted real. He squinted. "You okay, Aves?"

Ava nodded.

"Everything okay at work?"

"Yes."

He stared. "The kids okay?"

"Still sleeping."

"Tell me what's wrong."

But, how could she? What would she say? That she was stretched too thin? That she was trying to live a life in multiple dimensions but could only exist in a single one? That her role as a mother directly contradicted her role as a professional, that her role as a professional made her feel guilt for her failings as a mother? That her passion for freelance design taxed her marriage, and that her marriage took energy away from her creativity? That she had no idea who she was anymore? How could she begin to release the pressure of the flood of ideas raging in her mind and soul?

She looked down at the woman, still frozen at her feet.

"I think I just need some coffee," she said.

Mark nodded. "Okay, well I better start these taxes." He offered a smile. "I'll take a coffee if you're making it."

Ava nodded. Mark hurried away into the office.

"This isn't a dream," Ava told the woman.

The woman rose from the ground, turned on the coffee maker, and deposited the shards of the mug into the trash.

The outskirts of Ava's mind panicked. Her mind leapt from *Invasion of the Body Snatchers* to biological warfare to a personal psychotic break.

The coffee bubbled and brewed, and the woman pushed the button for a single serving. Ava watched, perplexed, as the coffee filled the mug the woman had placed there.

"Can you believe the kids are still sleeping?" Mark asked, reemerging from the office without his tax folder. He grabbed the coffee mug, came around to Ava, and kissed her neck from behind.

"Kids? Yeah, I guess so."

Mark raised an eyebrow. "You look like you just woke up." He looked around the kitchen. "It looks great in here, though." He kissed her again, then disappeared with his coffee into the office.

Ava spun around. Where had the woman gone? The noise of a tape dispenser at the dining room table drew Ava there. The woman was wrapping the gift for the birthday girl. Of course—Ava had forgotten about wrapping it. The woman set out the card they'd bought, placed a purple marker for Jenny to write her name with, and was already working on cleaning the dining room table from last night's dinosaur-clay-toy block escapades.

"I might… shower?" Ava said.

The woman nodded and continued cleaning, while Ava floated up the steps, knowing for sure this felt like a dream but knowing that dreams never felt this real. Maybe this was it. Maybe she had finally snapped.

Ava stayed under the water forever. She hadn't taken a shower that long since college. She at first decided she'd stay in the shower long enough for the weirdness to wash away, for reality to come back. She thought for sure either she'd wake up in bed, or if this were real, one of her kids would come tumbling into the bathroom, pounding on the glass shower door asking about breakfast or complaining about the other sibling not sharing or some other minor catastrophe, as they always did.

But no child came. She let the strange worry float away with the hot water. When she finished, she heard no sounds of fighting or urgency, so she treated her hair with several products, things she reserved only for the most important client meetings. And here she was doing it on a Saturday! She used a pumice-scrub on her foot and an invigorating face wash. It had been a Christmas gift years ago and was well past its expiration date, but it worked, nonetheless.

She stepped out of her bedroom refreshed, her skin tingling with cleanliness, and her muscles relaxed. She had almost forgotten about the woman.

Downstairs, the kids were seated quietly on the couch, eating freshly-baked blueberry muffins. They were watching a show on the streaming service. It was one Ava had never heard of, but somehow it managed to captivate both of them. And they were drinking some kind of smoothie?

In the kitchen, the woman placed a plate with a blueberry muffin next to a banana smoothie in a glass. She nodded, then left the room just as Mark entered again. He pulled Ava into his arms and planted a kiss on her lips. He tasted like blueberry and banana. "I'd forgotten what an amazing cook I married," he said, pulling her close. "It's been years since you made your famous blueberry muffins."

His passion turned Ava's confusion into a smile.

"Yeah, Mom. Breakfast is really good today."

It was true, the muffin looked tempting compared to the usual prepared grab-and-go food Ava kept on hand for the Morning Struggle.

"Okay, well... Jenny, don't forget about your party. We'll leave in an hour or so. And, Sammy, you're coming along. The weather's great, and we're meeting Mattias and his mom for a playdate at Springwood."

"Yay!" Sammy stuck his tongue out at Jenny. "Springwood's much more fun than some dumb party for *girls*."

"Yeah, well I get a goody bag, and you don't," Jenny spat back.

But the two quickly re-absorbed themselves in the show. Mark offered a departing kiss before returning to the office, and Ava sat at the counter, enjoying the sight of a clean kitchen while devouring the freshly-baked muffin. It had, indeed, been years since she'd baked them. Why had she ever stopped?

Later, with the kids buckled in the minivan, Ava returned inside. She told the kids she was going inside for her water bottle, but really, she needed to check on the woman lurking in the dining room. She found her instead at the kitchen sink, washing the few dishes that had been dirtied at breakfast.

"I don't know who you are," Ava whispered, eyeing the office. "Can you talk?"

The woman shook her head.

"Are you going to hurt us?"

The woman's eyes flashed open, and she shook her head.

"Are you an angel?"

The woman shrugged.

"Okay, well I don't know what your plan is, but I'm leaving for a few hours. Mark knows I'm leaving. If he sees you in here, things are going to get weird."

The woman stared blankly.

"Understand?"

The woman nodded.

Ava sighed and dashed out of the kitchen. She had one foot out the door when she shook her head and turned around. She nearly crashed into the woman, who was standing right there, holding Ava's forgotten water bottle out to her.

After the party and playdate and a dozen other errands, Ava drove home with the car full of take-out, groceries, and tired kids. Her head spun with an idea for the cake logo, and she tried to impress it in her mind so that she would not forget it later. As she set the newly-cleared dining room table with the spread of Chinese food containers, her phone vibrated. It was a text from the neighbor.

Nice job on the bushes, the text read.

Ava peered out the window. Indeed, the bushes were trimmed, the weeds were pulled. It looked like a professional landscaper had come through.

Thanks, Ava texted back.

I mean really, can I hire you ;)

Ava shook her head, remembering the first apartment she and Mark had in college. She had so much free time then, her front garden always looked like it belonged in a magazine. But now, weeding was the last thing on her mind. Like the house, the garden was usually a mess. Except now—

Speaking of, where was this woman? Ava peered at the garden. The sun was setting, and the pod plant looked different.

"Kids, you start eating. I'll be right back. Mark," she called. "Dinner in five!"

Ava patted her leg, instructing Benny to join her. The two sauntered out to the garden. The pod was closed now. It was huge, too heavy for the stalk, which bent until the pod touched the ground. The pod was rounder, fuller, than Ava remembered. It was large enough to encompass the body of a woman who might be curled into a ball, in the fetal position.

Ava shivered in the setting sun. Despite the creep factor, the scene really was beautiful. Maybe it was the nostalgia of the blueberry muffins, but Ava thought again to her days as an art student. Her creative inklings had been filled first by her children and then by her marketing career. But there was something about using her talents to sell chicken breasts or toilet paper that left the desire for more.

Benny nudged her leg, so she left the scene and hurried inside. There, Mark was unloading the groceries she had left on the counter.

"Got most of the taxes done," he said.

"Good."

"It is good. We don't owe anything this year. Maybe a small refund."

"Oh yeah?"

He nodded. "Maybe big enough to pay for dinner tonight." They both laughed, then walked to the dining room together, Mark touching the small of her back. A tingle rushed up her spine. Could the blueberry muffins be responsible for that nostalgia, too? How many years had it been since she'd felt that rush of passion? She almost couldn't wait to get the kids to bed.

Later, sleeping in Mark's arms, her bare skin on his, she woke to the moonlight. Sammy was fussing in his sleep again. Most kids slept through the night by now, but as the doctor said, some parents just got lucky.

Mark moaned. "Again?"

Ava groaned. "Maybe teething?"

"At this age?"

They ignored Sammy for a few minutes, as the doctor suggested, and he finally went back to sleep.

Mark turned sleepily toward Ava. "I meant to tell you. When I was looking for our box of medical receipts, I found that old portfolio."

"Portfolio?"

"The purple one. You know, with your sketch books and pencils and stuff. Forgot we still had that. Thought you might want to know..." His speech dissolved into snores, and Ava sat up in bed. She was wide awake, so she pulled on pajamas and socks and crept down to the office. It was only 2 a.m. So much more time before anyone rose and not an ounce of fatigue.

The case of colored pencils felt familiar and foreign all at once. It was a brown leather case, a gift from her grandmother for her high school graduation. The case was ancient, but it was real leather, well treated, and it held up to time. Inside were her pencils, just as she had left them. She picked one up, cerulean, and sucked in a breath. It was like an artifact. The last time she had held this she was—she wasn't even herself, was she? She wasn't a mother, a marketer, a wife. She was just—who?

She ran her fingers over the pencils, absorbing whatever power they seemed to retain. Then Ava went outside: pajamas, boots, jacket. She pulled a lawn chair in front of the garden, and she sketched, using her knees as an easel. The nearly full moon hung low on the horizon, a magical backdrop to the mysterious pod in the garden. She sketched it through a dream-colored lens. Instead of being weighted down, the pod on her page was weightless and stretched up into the sky.

When she finished, it wasn't yet 4 a.m., so she went inside to work on the cake logo. Before sunrise, she had seven rough sketches and three finalists. She sent them off in an email and waited for amazement.

The amazement did come, later that morning. A happy client and a paid invoice. With taxes done and the house relatively clean, the family went on an afternoon outing, going to a working historic farm. The afternoon got the kids dirty and tired, and after bath, Mark and Ava climbed into bed, enjoying freshly laundered sheets.

Ava turned and smiled at him instead of falling into a dead sleep.

"You're different," he said.

"How?"

"There's just this energy. I don't know. Like something's very right."

Ava shrugged. "The cake client loved my logo. He referred me to several other creatives who need design help. I guess being creative on my own energizes me."

Mark smiled. "I'm glad." He paused. "Why did you ever stop?"

It was a loaded question. How could she possibly even answer? Marriage, job, kids, chores? How could she possibly *not* have stopped? But she didn't want to get into the weeds, so she just shrugged. "I should do more, I guess."

"Yes," Mark said. "Yes, you should."

Ava turned off the lights and melted into him.

After work on Monday, Ava returned to find the playroom cleaned and all the bathrooms washed. In the refrigerator, chicken was marinating.

"What can we do?" Jenny asked, kicking off her shoes. "I'm bored." Normally, Ava would have asked Jenny to clean the playroom. Jenny would have put a few toys away, procrastinated, then complained until Ava did it herself. Without that battle, how would they spend the afternoon?

Ava turned on the oven. "I'll put this chicken in the oven, and maybe we can go for a walk? Or draw?"

"Let's paint," Jenny said.

They decided on a series of paintings. Ava lovingly called it "Alphabet soup." Each letter of the alphabet was illustrated as a different object. Sammy helped to paint, and Ava put on the finishing touches so that the letters each took on their own personality, morphing from Sammy's blobs.

Underneath each letter, Jenny carefully wrote the name of the food in calligraphic lettering she was apparently studying in art class. "'A' is for Angel," Jenny told her brother.

"What's an angel?" Sammy asked.

Ava remembered doing a project in college, a series of paintings, about angels. She had been startled to know that the etymology of the terms meant "messenger" and not "guardian," as she had thought. She learned that halfway through, and her angels changed for the second half of her project. They were more frightening, more powerful.

"It's a dead person that wears white all the time," Jenny explained. "With wings and halos and stuff."

"Oh." Sammy moved on. Ava stared out at the garden.

Sammy seemed amused by the project and for the first time took an interest in his letters.

For dinner, they cut up chicken into strips and made them into letter shapes on everyone's plates to help Sammy practice. After bedtime, Ava and Mark washed the dishes together—her washing, him drying—like they used to do so many years ago in their first apartment.

When they finished, Mark turned on the faucet and sprayed water on her, laughing.

"What the hell, Mark?" she asked. But then she saw his face.

"Better get you out of those wet clothes before you catch a cold," he said. An old line from college. They both laughed on the way up the stairs.

In the moonlight, the pod grew full and rested.

All spring, the woman came, adept at sneaking unnoticed. Ava came home to cleanliness and organization, and time. Jenny took a renewed interest in her brother, helping him with his alphabet, and Ava took to her sketchpad again, drawing at the request of both children, whose tidy rooms now bore on the walls dozens of sketches that fit their whimsy. Chimera football players, fairy princesses, dog-dragons walked by wizards.

And after the kids went to bed, Ava had the energy to devote to Mark. They chatted on the couch, they read the paper together, they went for starlit walks with Benny—though on these, Ava was always careful to direct him away from the garden and the strange pod.

The extra energy invigorated Ava at work. She finished projects quickly, with much less effort. She earned the Blue Star award from the firm's number two client for her work on their marketing campaign, and a small bonus along with it.

But what really made her smile was her freelance work. She loved working with clients one-on-one, using her creativity on their behalf. And really, she loved working at night. Something about the moonlight, the silence, allowed her creativity to blossom.

Even with the woman, the Morning Struggle was always too real. It was hard enough to focus on her own day, her schedule, her meetings with clients, let alone remember what Sammy had going on in preschool or what projects Jenny was working on. The rush out the door left her depleted and frazzled for the workday. And the woman, despite all her help, couldn't alleviate that.

"I'm much more myself," she told the woman who slept in her pod one cold September night. "And really I have you to thank. I'm sorry you have to do all the menial things. Granted, I never asked you to. Did I?"

Of course, the woman did not respond. In the distance, a fox cried.

"I'm stretched thin is the problem. Spread in too many directions. Jack of all trades kind of thing." The night was dark. The moon had sunk below the horizon. The faintest scent of decaying leaves hinted at autumn. "But what do I give up?"

She had more freelance work than she could handle, but the guaranteed salary and promised pension of her job was more than she'd like to abandon.

"You're leaving, though, aren't you?" The woman had done wonders. The cooking, the cleaning. Every scrap of clothing Ava had left to be mended or hemmed had been completed. But the woman was changing. She was moving more slowly, her hair graying with the drying grass. Autumn had started to color the leaves, and the woman's hair changed with it. Her eyes grew tired, colder. The pod was darker now, browner. More brittle.

The woman wouldn't last. And then what? Would things fall back into disrepair? Would Ava ignore Sammy and his strides in reading? Would she stop painting with Jenny? Would she and Mark exist as sleep-deprived robots once more, coexisting without actually living? Would each day become another list of chores?

And then there was her wait-list of clients. She was lucky to have more demand than time. Did she dare do what haunted the back of her mind? Another fox cried in the distance, and Ava shivered, whispered goodnight to the woman, and returned inside.

"I was thinking about early retirement," she told Mark.
"What?"

The two were lying in bed again, staring up at the ceiling. It was a cold night, the first frost, the first night they had to turn on the heat.

"I talked to HR. I have enough years in with the company to be vested. It won't be much, and the payments won't start for years, obviously, but I can take an early retirement package. There's even an option to purchase health coverage, you know, at retirement. If we need it."

Mark shook his head. "You know I get all that through my work."

Ava was quiet.

"Is this what you want? To be on your own is—terrifying. Constant."

"My work now is constant." *But in different directions, not unified.*

Mark groaned. "You have to work all the time to fight for clients. Your salary now comes automatically. On your own, nothing is guaranteed."

"Nothing is ever guaranteed," she said. She shied away from him.

Mark stared at her. She watched herself in his eyes. What was he seeing?

"I did the math. I can easily make up my current salary if I keep up the level of clients I have pounding on my door now. You know my work. It speaks for itself."

Mark licked his lips.

Silence.

"What are you thinking?" she asked.

Mark's expression melted into a smile. "I was just thinking about college."

"What about it?"

"You don't remember, do you?"

"Remember what?"

"Why you didn't take the art cooperative."

"Art cooperative?"

"I didn't think you remembered. In college, when we were picking schedules for our senior year. One of the options you had was some kind of art cooperative. I forget what they called the actual course, but the gist was, you worked in some kind of makerspace in which you were paired with community members. People from the community would apply to be partnered with someone from the college, and students would create art for them."

"It rings a bell."

"It was right up your alley. Using creative talents to help those around you. It's truly what you were made for. You didn't sign up, though. Do you remember why?"

Ava shook her head. "I barely remember the class, let alone why I didn't take it."

"It met at 8 a.m. is the first thing."

"I never was a morning person."

"But it also required you to give up your Friday nights to do a community outreach event with the partners. Good networking. Job prospects. I was greedy. I talked you out of it. You don't remember, do you?"

"You... talked me out of it?"

Mark pushed himself up with one elbow. "I'm sorry about it now, now that I see how much you love doing this kind of thing. But back then, I was being selfish. I wanted you to myself on Friday nights. I didn't want to compete with your love of art. When you mentioned that the class met early in the morning, I helped you remember how much you hate mornings. I could have kept my mouth shut. Or maybe even talked you into it. I didn't want to marry someone who was already married to her work."

Ava's mind raced. "What are you saying?"

"What I'm saying is, I held you back once already. If you want to go full-freelance, then I'm behind you one hundred percent." Mark kissed her forehead. "If that's what you want."

It is. She kissed him goodnight and waited until his breathing steadied. Then she went down to the living room to sketch by moonlight.

What would it be like to email clients at midnight? To tackle the Morning Struggle in her PJs, if she felt like it? The days would be hers to tend to the house, and the night hours would be hers to be creative.

With several weeks' notice, she left her work before Thanksgiving. The frost had taken her garden, and on a cold Saturday in November, she went out to clear it while the kids watched a movie with Mark. The pod was still there, full, but its bulk was light, like the essence of what was inside had shriveled away. The woman had not been out for two weeks, and Ava knew.

The stems from tomato and cucumber and pumpkin she pulled to the compost heap until the garden was cleared—all except the pod. She pulled gently on the twin stalks, which came away easily, relinquishing their hold in the soil. She rocked it like a child, gently nestling it to her chest. She carried it away from the garden, away from the compost.

In the corner of the yard was a flower garden. It was something new, something she had created while the kids were at school this week, based on a design she had sketched in college. It was bare now, but in the spring, the bulbs she planned to plant would flourish. For now, she placed the husk on the lawn and gently dug out the garden with her spade. When the hole was long enough, and deep, she placed the dried husk inside.

"Thank you," she said. An owl hooted in the distance, and Ava smiled down at her garden before heading inside to email a client.

ARIANNA SEBO

Biography

Arianna Sebo (she/her) is a poet and writer living in Southern Alberta with her husband, pug, and five cats. Their home is brimming with cat posts, pet beds, fur, and love. She received her B.A. in philosophy from the University of Calgary, working in the field of law to feed her family and writing poetry to feed her philosophical soul. Her poetry can be found in *Kissing Dynamite*, *The Coachella Review*, *Front Porch Review*, and *45 Poems of Protest: The Pandemic*. Follow her at AriannaSebo.com and @AriannaSebo on Twitter and Instagram.

Arianna Sebo

THE ACTRESS WITH THE RED HAIR

I get tired of seeing
the same woman
in the same roles
over and over again
before we know it she'll
be 80 and still playing
smart sassy women with
great hair
which is fine
really
but sometimes it's nice to
witness an actress
challenge herself
and become something more
than what she once
was

Arianna Sebo

MOODY GIRL

How to change a mood
without drowning in its
after-effects
being caught in its lethargic
waters
no release
sucking you down to the depths
of all emotions
dying to swallow you whole
What kind of mess have you
gotten yourself into?
Depression doesn't suit you
Time to up your meds

Arianna Sebo

REELING

It's nice seeing people you
knew from high school
you get to see how they've
aged; what they're doing
these days
then it reminds you how
you've aged
how you've changed
and if your life is going well
it doesn't stress you out
but if you're at all unsure
about your place in the world
this meeting of chance could
send you reeling

C. MARRY HULTMAN

Biography

C. Marry Hultman is a teacher, writer and sometimes podcaster who is equal parts Swede and Wisconsinite. He lives with his wife and two daughters and runs W.A.R.G –The Guild podcast dedicated to interviewing authors about their creative process. In addition to that, he runs the website Wisconsin Noir – Cosmic Horror set in the Dairy State where he collects short fiction and general thoughts. His work has been featured in several anthologies. Find out more about him at https://wisconsinnoir.wixsite.com/wisnoir or he can be found on Twitter @stoughe or Facebook @WisconsinNoir.

C. Marry Hultman

IF YOU SEE ME WAVE

The whistle blew a second time, and Erik took one last drag on his cigarette before tossing it on the platform. He put the dog-eared copy of Metro 2033 in his backpack, slung it over his shoulder, and patted his jean pocket to make sure his wallet was in place. He noticed that the conductor gave that final look up and down to see if any stragglers were running up the stairs from the underground tunnel. Erik noticed a few men in business attire, carrying briefcases come bounding upward, with a panicked look in their eyes and knew he had a few minutes to spare. He had wanted to be the last one to climb onboard to avoid the bottleneck of bodies trying to find their seats. His backpack stuck out enough to knock most people over when he tried to traverse the sea of humanity. It was something he had discovered when taking the train from Penn Station to D.C. the previous year. Much to the dismay of an older man, who cursed and then promptly vanished without giving Erik the chance to apologize.

The train doors closed with a deafening sound, something between the creak of an unoiled door and someone scraping a fork against a plate. Luckily, he had his earbuds in, and they softened the noise. The third whistle blew, and the train moved from the station. It had begun. He was leaving Copenhagen, and with only one change of trains in Hamburg, he would soon be in Bremen.

His attempt to avoid the disoriented people looking for their seats had failed. To his dismay, he found that several passengers were still standing. He sighed and leaned on the door to the washroom and tried to appreciate the comedy played out before him. Once most of the confusion had settled, he made his move. The narrow aisle still created some difficulty, and the few elderly Danes who were trying to decide

39

what items they wanted with them from their bags, were like icebergs to the Titanic. He had his phone in his hands and opened the email with his travel information. He found his seat; 32B, it was an aisle seat, but the window one was empty, and since the train was already moving, he felt confident he could claim it. He let the backpack fall onto the seat at the same time he did, he had practiced it several times when he was a kid, and now it was just another thing he did. It was part of his identity. Like the black skinny jeans and T-shirt, he wore and the matching nail polish on his right hand. The train passed through a longer tunnel, and it gave him the opportunity to check his reflection in the window. He pulled his hand through the mass of light brown hair on his head and moved it to his left side. Why? He would be travelling for almost six hours, what he looked like to others did not matter here. For some reason the sense of always being judged was difficult to shake. He leaned back, closed his eyes, and felt his body becoming one with the train. His spirit moving with it.

He was too antsy to fall asleep. He was finally doing it. Was at last going somewhere. Finding a place where he could be himself, not who others needed him to be. Erik thought back, a year ago he had been sitting in his father's tractor. Sipping coffee he had brought with him in a thermos and feeling empty inside. The emptiness was like an old friend, part of the family even. His mother had felt it when her husband spiraled deep into depression; it held his sister as she leaned over the toilet, and here it was, standing in a field, staring at him. Then he had assumed he was going insane; manic maybe, seeing things. His six months of psychology studies at university had given him all the wrong tools to analyze his own mind. The emptiness looked like him, a skinny boy recently turned twenty, dressed like the other bumpkins in the village; trucker hat, flannel shirt and light blue, stained and torn jeans. Dip in his cheek and spitting brown liquid at short intervals. Brown teeth smiling.

'Just give in' it said. 'This is your future here. Like all your childhood friends, I have already convinced to stay. Give up the pretense of equality and be like the rest.'

At that moment it was as if two pathways opened up, awaiting his decision.

He had been on his way to becoming what the village wanted him to be. He had never realized that there was anything else out there. He went to the movies with his friends, they watched entertaining high school comedies, fart movies his mother called them, drove round the city square on their mopeds and drank moonshine on the weekends.

That evening he had spoken to his mother in the kitchen. She was washing dishes as he was leaning on the laminate-topped island.

'Mom, I think I'm ready to go to school.' He said in a soft tone, walking on eggshells.

'I'm happy to hear that.' She said, not looking at him. 'It is about time.'

'If it's okay with you and dad.' He continued, ignoring her words.

'Why wouldn't it be?' She was paying more attention to the soapy water than to him.

'I mean, will you guys be okay without me?' He was trying to hammer home the question. He felt she was evading it.

The conversation had been quite different a year earlier. He had graduated high school and felt the pull of the world outside. From being quite skeptical when it came to learning, another gift from his village, where such things were frowned upon. If it did not have anything to do with crops or the paper factory, which kept the place running, it was of no importance.

C. Marry Hultman

He had left for a charter school instead of joining his friends at the local house of learning. It had created somewhat of a stir, and a rift, but he felt he needed to be some place where the emptiness would not find him. The introduction to a different environment had been tough on him. Suddenly he met youngsters who cared about the way they dressed. They did not read auto mags; instead, they read books about people long since deceased. They did not go to the movies they went to the theatre. It was a different world. Gone were days of opening the boot of your car, drinking moonshine from glass jars while laughing at those who did not fit in. Instead, it was red wine round a kitchen table, discussing social and political issues. He realized how little he knew of the world and how he had needed those conversations. The change had been welcome, and he felt he could be himself for once. Things came easy to him and he aced the subjects until second year. It had been like hitting a brick wall and he struggled, and the emptiness was there again. It would sit with him in the classroom, in study hall, at lunch. It would smile at him and whisper in his ear:

'Go back home.' It whispered, 'There is work to be done at the farm.'

He kept his head down, confided in his teachers, for his parents could not help, and once he graduated, he had found the thirst for knowledge again. As he stood on the stage and received his diploma, he could see that familiar shape, standing behind his parents, grinning.

'You know we are struggling right now, Erik.' His mother had said then. He had just broached the subject of going off to university. He had sighed because this was the answer he had expected.

C. Marry Hultman

'I have to work full time, your father just left his job to run the farm, and your sister... ' She could not bring herself to say it.

His sister. Three years his junior, she was the apple of his eye. The village, with its young boys, their judgmental attitude and coarse language. It had eaten her whole. School enabled it. The teachers could not tame them of their wild ways. The poor girls were trod on. Realizing that they would not be heard in the classroom. Some resigned themselves to that life and went into relationships with those same boys. Moving from partner to partner, having children with various men, and settling into a loveless life. Some fled and moved to bigger cities, hoping to leave it all behind, but old habits die hard and the subjugation often followed them. Yet others, like his sister, remained and crumbled like old industrial buildings on the outskirts. She wilted. The poor delicate flower. The emptiness crept inside her and created a black hole and she starved herself.

At night, he could hear her through the wall they shared. Throwing up and crying. He would turn to his side, only to be met by the emptiness who would stare at him and grin.

His father had worked with his brother in the family business. A mill they had inherited from their parents. The brothers did not get along and they were constantly at each other's throats. His father was a sensitive type and the years of conflict took its toll. Erik could see him being worn down as the years passed and the old man went into a deep depression. One day he sold his share of the company and he walked away. The family had always had a bit of farmland, but now his father put everything into the venture. His father's demeanor changed to begin with. It was as if a great weight had lifted from his shoulders, but then reality hit. He had spent the buyout and all the family savings on the equipment and grains. He could ill afford to hire hands to help him out. This was the most important part of his mother's concerns once he had voiced his wishes to move on.

'We need you too much right now.' His mother continued. 'Your father would send you away without a second thought, but you know how he is. He does not talk. I always wanted something different for you. I wanted you to communicate with us, telling us everything.'

She evaded the significant part again, but her message was clear, they needed him. Once again, his mother had to be the voice to say so because she was the only one who dared to. He stayed and worked on the farm, supported his sister and helped his mother when she needed it. He gave freely of himself to his family and they took, without giving back. As the weeks became months, and the seasons changed he felt increasingly hollow inside. Every morning, when he had to get up at dawn to feed the animals or clean the barn, every conversation with his mother, trying to reassure her he wasn't leaving and every night he stayed in his sister's room keeping her from running to the bathroom to throw up. He tried to fill the void and combat the emptiness by starting a band. A punk rock outfit with three guys with an abundance of social zeitgeist. He screamed his angst into the microphone, to a not so pleased crowd. It was not enough.

'It's ok now son.' His mom relented. 'It's time to go do what's best for you' and in that moment he had realized it was true. His family had drained him. His sister had gotten the help she needed and was on her way to get better. The hard graft on the farm had yielded an income, his father had hired more hands, and his mother was smiling again. Therefore, it was decided, he could leave, and he did so. He moved south, three hours away by train. He studied psychology and did well. The classes, lectures and discussions satiated his thirst for knowledge, and he was happy for the first time in a long time.

The train slowed, and a platform came into view. His reminiscing had caused him to lose track of time. He looked around, only to find people minding their own business. Lost in their tablets or e-readers, Sudoku or crossword puzzles. It was fine by him; he had little need of social interaction now.

He had learned so much during the six months he had spent at that university. It had given him a deeper understanding of his family, and his own situation. Why he needed to be alone in old abandoned buildings, or why he was doomed to ruin every relationship he had ever had. The freedom from his family caused him to act out and run wild. Soon the studies made way for all night benders and one-night stands. It had all started when he failed his first assignment. As soon as he was handed his result the emptiness was in his ear, standing beside him. *I knew you'd fail*. It said. *Who were you trying to kid by trying to better yourself?* His debauchery was an attempt at drowning that voice out. It only resulted in him waking up with anxiety, destitute and with some form of horrible rash on his privates. So, he dropped the studies and went back home to detox and use the salve he had received from the doctor and the emptiness waited for him at the end of his parent's driveway. Arms extended and with a smile on its face.

This time his family took care of him while he recovered. He worked at a mill, loading bags of flour on to trucks. Slowly his brain repaired itself, as he spent his evenings in his sister's lap, watching TV. Then one day, as they were watching Anthony Bourdain's No Reservations, it came to him. Bourdain had traveled to Germany and was partaking in the culinary delights of Berlin when Erik realized what he needed.

'Why, Bremen?' His mother had asked as they once again cleaned up after dinner.

'Well, I did study German in high school.' He had replied. 'And I just really need to get out of here. I need to see the world.'

The rest of the year, he continued to work at the mill, breaking his back under bags of flour, collecting money. It cost him a pretty penny for one year of studies, complete with living expenses, but the hard work paid off. Then one day, he was standing on the platform, getting ready to head out into the world.

He was roused by something. He noticed that he was no longer alone; someone was sitting next to him, or rather something.

'Hi there.' The emptiness said and smiled. It was wearing blue coveralls, stained with dirt and grime. 'Running again?'

'Not really.' Erik replied and looked out the window, only to be met by those eyes reflected back at him.

'Interesting, cause from where I sit, it looks like it.'

'I'm tired of you.' Erik felt so confused that he did not know if he was speaking or if the conversation was in his head. 'I have realized that there is no point in running. It might be a cliché, but there is truth to it.'

'So, you think you can rise above your station. You're trash, you've always been and will always be. Nothing you ever do will change that; there is no point in trying to better yourself.'

C. Marry Hultman

'My background and my family will always be part of who I am. It has molded me, and I would be a fool to deny it. It's not about rising above anything; it's about owning it and making the best of things. It took a long time for me to come to terms with it. You had some small part in that, I must admit.'

'Thank you.' The emptiness smiled again.

'But I think it's time we part ways. I am certain you'll find me again. Our paths will cross again. You will always be there in the background to remind me of who I am, or where I came from.'

The train pulled into one of the stops on the way. The emptiness gave Erik a sideways glance and appeared to be pondering something. It shrugged and gave him a wink. Then it rose and walked off. As the train once again pulled away from the platform, he could see it through the window, standing there, hands in pockets. Erik picked up his phone and pulled out the little note his sister had left him in a pocket meant for credit cards. He unfolded it and read:

Thank you for letting me borrow your jacket; it kept me warm in a cold place.

SIMA GREENFIELD

    Sima Greenfield is originally from Albuquerque, NM. Now she's living in Los Angeles, CA as a Marketing Coordinator for an event production company. Her writing has been featured in Wave Journey, Bound, and Thought Catalog. In her free time, she hikes, crafts, and goes to art galleries.

Sima Greenfield

Haunted House

If I was a haunted house
    My ghosts would be pranksters because they're bored.
        They would laugh in your ear, so you spill your coffee.
        They would open doors to get your attention.
        They would change the song just to let you know they're there.
    Every room would be filled with a strange feeling but not a bad feeling.
It would be strange enough to warrant a ghost hunter but not an exorcism.

If I was a haunted house,
    I would be housing other people's choices that I have to live with.
        It would echo all the bad news I had to take on.
        The drops of the bath water overflowing into the hall.
        The whisper of, "You need to use the knife so I can go to heaven."
        The crash of my head into the desert sands.
    The residual energy of choices past.
Particles charged by bearing witness.

The spirits aren't mad. They simply exist.
    Each memory:
        Residue on floorboards.
        Vibrations in the hollow walls.
        Musty smells, antique fixtures.
    Parts making a whole.
Pieces coming together to house a life.

If I was a haunted house my style would be shabby chic.
    Each piece of decor representing significant time.
        Meals had.
        Lover's kisses.
        Tears from laughing.
    My ghosts are happy to be in light
But aware of the darkness.

BOBBI SINHA-MOREY

Biography

Bobbi Sinha-Morey's poetry has appeared in a wide variety of places such as Plainsongs, Pirene's Fountain, The Wayfarer, Helix Magazine, Miller's Pond, The Tau, Vita Brevis, Cascadia Rising Review, Old Red Kimona, and Woods Reader. Her books of poetry are available at Amazon.com, and her work has been nominated for Best of the Net in 2015 and the Best of the Net 2018 Anthology Awards hosted by Sundress Publications. Her website is located at https://bobbisinhamorey.wordpress.com/

Bobbi Sinha-Morey

No Bright Star

Every day I wake up I feel
so cold, see the faraway sun
press its icy chill to the window,
reminded of an uncaring god
who left me here, a house on
a hill, ruled over by a witch
I never wanted for a mother,
watchful of my every move
who thought I should take
happy pills, crept every room
by day while I would cloak
my only mirror with a dark
cloth just so I wouldn't see
my face in hers; the only trace
of myself a gentle strength in
my face, a tiny flame inside
my heart that never dies out.
The only thoughts I ever
wrote down were in the pages
of my diary torn out by my
mother's malicious hand and
burnt to the quick; no whisper
of my past to point a finger at
my abuser, no bright star to light
the empty sky. It's only when
I sleep I find myself dying,
the broken curve of a halo
circling itself around my lost
dreams.

Bobbi Sinha-Morey

Sara

I saw her slip away down
the steps of the porch; Sara,
a woman in her seventies,
always quant to be with,
never willing to breathe in
any dark emotion, whose
orison she aimed at the sky
to reach the goodness in
heaven. A lady so pretty for
her age with her white blonde
hair curled under who slowly,
barely recovered having lost
her husband over the years.
I imagined herself once so
introverted and shy, taking
forever to open up. She'd
come to be at ease with us,
the social hub on the block,
and in her delicate condition
she was always so careful
about living a low-key life:
no negative ions, no carriers
of bad news, but the glow
inside of Sara always made
her pleasant to be around.
She loved the world that
always swayed to its own
joy, wrapped her in its soft
arm of sleep.

Bobbi Sinha-Morey

On The Fourth Day

Days had gone by that his
white truck hadn't been
there, our neighbor Gerry
gone to see his wife in the
hospital with broken bones
in her vertebrae, dementia
eating her away, a meek
woman in her seventies,
and how long she'd last
I didn't know. The thought
of her dying preyed on me
in the night and I'd barely
slept when dawn started
to creep in through the
blinds. On the fourth day
I saw him come home;
above, silent clouds. And
in the dusty light that shined
through his kitchen window
he was yelling angrily into
the phone. I'd felt the knot
and twist of each muscle
that must've been growing
inside of him; and in the
minutes of the coming
dusk, gnats rose in their
erratic flight. It was then,
peering through the window,
I'd seen his chin quiver and
it was the first time I'd ever
seen a man cry. Heaven had
silently opened its door.

KASISI HARRIS

Biography

K. D. Harris holds a B.S. in General Engineering from the United States Naval Academy and a B.F.A. in Creative Writing for Entertainment from Full Sail University.

Publications to his credit include "For If They Fall...," (Down in the Dirt Magazine, July 2018), and "Turbulence," (The Corvus Review, July 2018).

He's served as an enlisted member of the United States Navy and a Commissioned Officer in the United States Marine Corps. A tattoo on his back pays tribute to the words of Ralph Waldo Emerson, "To know even one life can breathe easier because you have lived...".

Follow K. D. Harris at www.kasisiharris.com

Can't Take It Back: A Coming Out Story

Once you've posted it, you can't take it back. The thought paralyzed me. My knees bounced up and down as if keeping pace with an Olympic sprinter. My hands were shaking as I twirled my class ring around my finger. *What if everyone at work finds out? What'll they think of me?* My knees stopped dancing a jig, and my back straightened. I snapped out of my victim-like trance. *I won't shrink from this moment, not again.*

I remember the day I was weighed, measured, and found wanting. It was noon. Most people would've described the weather as hot. Hot is a word used to describe something that might cause a moment of discomfort; hot soup, a hot stove, or being hot and bothered. Agony, or my personal favorite, the seventh level of hell, better described the desert's noonday temperatures in Twentynine Palms, California. You pray for anything that can cool you; shade of a tree, a passing cloud, or if god is merciful, air conditioning. All the Company Grade Officers stood outside waiting for the base chapel to open its doors. I stood near the entrance with Shorty, a fellow Marine and Naval Academy classmate. We chatted idly as another Marine approached us. Our class rings glinted in the sun like signal beacons. They were gaudy. Yet, to the Naval Academy graduate, they represented years of long hours, overcome obstacles, and the accomplishment of a goal that not many could share.

"Hey!" The Marine immediately shook Shorty's hand.

"Look at this slacker. Kaz, this is Craig," Shorty said.

Marines come in all shapes and sizes. Shorty and Craig were the short, lean, and scrappy type; all muscle and not an ounce of fat. We continued our idle banter. I learned that Craig had a wife, and a brand new baby boy. In the middle of our conversation the doors to the chapel opened and we made our way inside.

The sweat from our bodies evaporated in the cool air. The air-conditioned space was like drinking an ice cold beverage on a sunbaked day. Shorty spotted some Officers from his Command, said his goodbyes, and joined them. Craig and I headed to the front of the chapel. The camouflaged congregation crowded into the hard wooden pews and awaited our four-star Jesus, the Commandant of the Marine Corps. Around me, I heard the normal rumblings of my peers catching up with friends from other units on base and speculating as to what the Commandant would say. We all knew what the Town Hall was about. The Military's policy of Don't Ask, Don't Tell had just been repealed. Under that policy, a homosexual was not permitted to share their sexuality in any capacity. Doing so, made them subject to discharge from the military. The acting Commandant had made his dissent of the repeal well known. To him, the integration of openly homosexual troops into the Marine Corps had the "potential for disruption" (Mulrine, 2010). And, like loyal Marines, none of us opposed this view without intense scrutiny from our Commanders and our peers. How your Commanders and peers viewed you was everything in the Marines. Perception, for all intents and purposes, was reality.

Like most of my homosexual counterparts, I hid in plain sight simply by not discussing sexual matters at all (Jackson & Smolowe, 1993). My work was my priority. As a result, people considered me focused and a hard charger. They even considered it rude to discuss such lewd sexual topics in my presence. However, that day in the base chapel, my disguise began to come undone. The subject matter weighed on me so heavy it was difficult to concentrate. I couldn't walk away. I sat in silence and avoided eye contact with anyone. I feared everyone would see right through me. I wanted to shrink, to hide, to disappear. I clutched my class ring, spinning it around my finger. My heart was pounding. I kept my eyes focused straight ahead on the altar until the General arrived.

"Attention on Deck!" a voice commanded.

We stood as the Commandant made his entrance. And at the Commandant's command, we sat. The Commandant said a great many things that day, most of which I don't remember. However, before he parted, he asked one question.

"How many of you would be willing to serve side-by-side with homosexuals?"

The room was silent. I could feel the heat coming off my ears. I knew in this moment I should raise my hand. I'm a homosexual, and I had served my country honorably, side-by-side with heterosexuals for years. However, my arms were glued to my sides. *If I raise my hand, they'll think I'm gay. My Command would...*

In that moment, I saw a single arm raise in front of me. It was Craig's arm. He was bold, unafraid, and alone in his show of support for a community that he didn't even belong to. I was dumbfounded. I wasn't even brave enough to stand up for myself. The Commandant said nothing in acknowledgment of the raised arm but was re-affirmed in his conviction by the overwhelming lack of raised arms. He thanked us for our time, and we stood to attention as he departed.

Craig and I never spoke again after that day. But his raised arm, at a time when I was too much of a coward to raise my own, is etched into my memory. I vowed, that when the time came again, I would not shrink from that moment. I would be brave, like Craig was brave.

In fact, the image of his raised arm was mentally with me as I sat in front of my laptop. I took a deep breath in. I straightened the class ring on my finger. *Once you've posted it, you can't take it back. They'll all know.* I clicked the left mouse button and watched the words take their position on my profile's wall:

Kasisi Harris

I thought long and hard about whether writing this was the right thing to do. I've determined that, public opinion aside, writing this is the right thing to do for me. In order to grow into the best version of myself, I've decided to be transparent. I'm gay. I know that some of you on my friends list may not approve of this. I know that some of you may be disappointed because in some way your perception of me has changed. If either of those are the case, please understand that it was not my intention to disappoint you in any way. If, because of your beliefs, you find it in your best interest to no longer be associated with me, I understand and respect that. I value whatever time we have interacted. And, I hope that the nature of our interaction is a good memory instead of a bad one. I would ask that you please unfriend me. However, before you do, know that if you should ever need me, simply contact me. If you're within my list of friends, it means that in some way I care for you and that doesn't change because we have different life opinions.

If you choose to stay, I ask for your help in this stage of my life. True friends are hard to find, and even harder to keep. And, I've always tried to bring honor to my family, and not disgrace it. I ask, whether family or friend, that you stand firm by me, as I will stand firm by you.

There it is. Written. Out. And, I can't take it back, nor do I want to. (Harris, 2018)

I closed my laptop. Finally, I was free.

References

Harris, K. [Kasisi]. (2018). (2018, June 20). Personal Post. Retrieved from https://www.facebook.com/kasisi.harris/timeline

Jackson, D. & Smolowe, J. (1983). Sex, lies, and the military. *TIME*, 141(6), 29 – 30. Retrieved from Academic Search Complete.

Mulrine, A. (2010). Not so fast on 'don't ask, don't tell' repeal, say top Pentagon brass. *Christian Scientist Monitor*, PAG. 1p.

BRUCE MCRAE

Biography

Bruce McRae, a Canadian musician currently residing on Salt Spring Island BC, is a multiple Pushcart nominee with over 1,600 poems published internationally in magazines such as *Poetry*, *Rattle* and the *North American Review*. His books are 'The So-Called Sonnets' (Silenced Press); 'An Unbecoming Fit Of Frenzy'; (Cawing Crow Press); 'Like As If' (Pski's Porch); 'Hearsay' (The Poet's Haven).

Bruce McRae

Actual Event

The night the roof blew off.
The night a very angry wind
stormed our homely little town.
The couple in bed, cuddling and warm,
dreaming of billy goats and peppermint,
who were suddenly woken
by a starry vista revealed overhead,
a mighty gust roaring its disapproval,
complaining vociferously,
Betelgeuse looking down on them,
nodding and winking surreptitiously,
as if in on a wicked secret.
And the couple drifting back to sleep,
which I think was unexpected.

Bruce McRae

Crow And The Songbirds

One day all the songbirds
gathered in the forest to complain
about crow, a cheeky bird, a bully bird,
a bird so bold as to even challenge
the two-legged ones who walked on ground.

Crow, complained the robin, is dark.
None of us can see him in the night.
He steals whatever he covets, the oriole sang.
And worst of all, the mockingbird chirped,
crow has no good song, he cannot sing.
His voice is a like a stick being broken
and therefore he is not beautiful.

Overhearing this, crow flew down
from the high branches to state his case.
Songbirds, said crow, who was naturally annoyed,
I have a voice but have only one song.
One song to sing, and only to sing it once.

See how crow is also a liar, countered the finch.
Angry, crow said then I shall sing my song
and prove to you the glory of my creation.
And crow sang a song so melodious, so lovely,
all the songbirds were silenced and amazed.
Some were so ashamed they wept openly
for the song of songs crow sang to them.

When crow had finished singing his one song
the others sat in silence, too stunned to apologize.
Then, with a huff, crow spread his wings and flew away,
cawing and cawing, admonishing the songbirds a last time.
And this is why the crow never sings today.
Having used his song he can only laugh or cough.
A moment of pride and his voice had gone.
He had wasted his gift and fed the silence.

Bruce McRae

Forgetful

I've got a memory like a wet bag.
Like a baffled bishop.
Like a popped lightbulb.

O metaphor. O simile.
My memory is a lukewarm broth
of roots and rabbit-water.
A gathered knot of alpaca's wool.
A runaway neutrino.

Imagine a cup of ambrosia,
then spilling its contents –
that's my memory.
Compare it to a dark alley
in the hard part of town.
A cobwebbed mausoleum.
A drunk's last dollar.

My memory is a guest star
in the constellation Cassiopeia.
It's a flower without a name
or clot of darkened matter.

And it resembles something else as well,
a thing beyond recall.
The ultimate fiction.

EDWARD LEE

Biography

Edward Lee's poetry, short stories, non-fiction and photography have been published in magazines in Ireland, England and America, including The Stinging Fly, Skylight 47, Acumen and Smiths Knoll. His debut poetry collection "Playing Poohsticks On Ha'Penny Bridge" was published in 2010. He is currently working towards a second collection. He also makes musical noise under the names Ayahuasca Collective, Lewis Milne, Orson Carroll, Blinded Architect, Lego Figures Fighting, and Pale Blond Boy. His blog/website can be found at https://edwardmlee.wordpress.com

Fool

At first Dean does not understand what Lucy is saying, then he is distracted by the almost childish glee in her eyes as the seemingly nonsensical words leave her mouth. The realization of what those words actually mean, when it comes, is brutal, as is the pain which follows swiftly, piercing his heart as though a hot spike has been hammered through his chest.

He rises from his chair, knocking it over in his haste; the sound it makes is like an echo of the sudden roaring which fills his ears. For a moment fear shows on Lucy's face, as though she believes he is about to strike her, and, God help him, he feels his own savage glee seeing that fear squeeze her beautiful features. It is a fleeting feeling, yes, but it is there, burning almost as hot as the pain her words have caused, and for the first time he finds himself wondering if any of the many horrible accusations she has levelled at him, in this very room over these past three months, might not hold some semblance of truth.

Disgusted that he has even given it any consideration, no matter how brief, he casts the thought away; all he can focus on is getting out of the room and rushing to the toilet down the end of the long corridor, before the contents of his stomach can burst from his mouth, the watery tell-tale hint already tickling the back of his throat.

He makes it, barely, his body spasming as he falls hard onto his knees and vomits into the toilet bowl. His eyes blur as he presses his hands against either side of the cubicle, his body breaking out in a cold sweat as it empties itself of everything but the words his soon-to-be ex-wife just spoke to him: "She isn't yours."

When Dean opens the door he sees his chair is still overturned on the ground. Lucy and Noelle, the mediator, are still sitting in their own chairs. They turn to look at him as he stands in the doorway, his hand on the handle, Lucy's face a mixture of triumph and what he might once have called regret, back before all this began, back before he discovered she was incapable of feeling such a thing, while Noelle's face is as impassive as it has been during all their mediation sessions.

He enters the room and closes the door gently behind him, his hand shaking as it lifts from the reassuring solidity of the handle. He rights his chair and sits down. It feels like he has been gone from the room for hours, when in fact it cannot have been any more than five minutes. The air feels changed, heavier than it was before, though he would not have thought such a thing possible, the tension in the room almost a fourth person, a silent witness to the dismantling of a marriage; it feels charged, primed to erupt in flame, the slightest word or gesture all the spark needed. He shouldn't have returned, even if by staying away he'd end up giving Lucy more ammunition to use against him, and, in her twisted portrayal of their marriage, more proof of his failings as a husband and a human being. He should have simply left the building when he had finished vomiting, and thought himself steady enough to stand and walk to the sinks where he splashed cold water on his face, avoiding looking at his reflection, fearful that he would not look as he once had, having just lost the only thing in the world he has left to care about.

She isn't yours.

He had goaded her, poked at her, intending to hurt her with his words of surety. He wanted to hold up a mirror and reveal her reflection cracked by all her infidelities. He wanted her to see how he now saw her. He *needed* to hurt her. He wanted to see, if only for a second, some pain on her face equal to all the pain she had inflicted upon him. He was not proud of this need, but neither was he made uncomfortable by it. Nor did he consider that by wanting to hurt her in this way he was proving her accusations true; it was simply a natural, almost instinctive, reaction to all she had done to him. It could be construed as a violent act, yes, maybe, but if it was, it was a violent act without the violence.

"After all your affairs, I'm lucky I know Jennifer is mine," he had said, sticking it into her like a knife, a knife he knew could not wound him. Jennifer their daughter, who looked like him, who acted like him in so many ways, who could be no one else's child but his own. Jennifer, *his* daughter, without any doubt, even when set beside all the affairs Lucy had conducted throughout their entire marriage, one of them occurring around the time she became pregnant with Jennifer, the knowledge of *all* her deceits only making themselves known to him in the aftermath of their break-up, as such things seem to do when there is no longer any need to weave and maintain the myriad of lies such affairs need to continue unnoticed, when the adulterer has no further cause, or desire, to spare your feelings.

"She isn't yours," Lucy had said, quickly, so very quickly, as if she had been waiting for a long time to say it, possibly ever since Jennifer had been born, waiting for an opening to slide those words, or some variation of them, into him - her own knife, sharpened into invisibility - waiting for him to speak the words he had spoken, or, again, some variation of them, making the task easier for her, just as he had made it easier for her to end their marriage when he, after being aware of it for two months and unable to hold it within himself anymore, confronted her about what he believed was her first and only affair.

She isn't yours.

Before those three words he hadn't believed his heart could be broken more than it already was. But hasn't he thought that several times since discovering Lucy had been having an affair, those first breath-stealing cracks appearing, then widening, deepening, until finally shards of his heart began to fall away? Didn't he eventually fool himself into finding much needed comfort in the surety that he could not feel any worse? And here he was, wrong again; whatever small, microscopic corner of his heart that had been left undamaged - the part, he imagined, that belonged to his daughter, that probably only still existed *because* of her - has just been destroyed into nothingness with the fact that his daughter is not his daughter.

He realizes that they are looking at him, Lucy and Noelle. Are they waiting for him to speak? Maybe they are. The last words spoken in the room were by Lucy, and his response had been to rush out and vomit. But what can he say? What can be said after such a revelation? His entire marriage, already so savagely rewritten by the knowledge of Lucy's affairs, has now been utterly, irrevocably voided. All those yesterdays that might as well not have existed. It almost feels like his marriage is being ended all over again, but this time with the deep, shuddering pain doubled, trebled.

He thinks of this coming weekend. It is meant to be his weekend with Jennifer. He has been looking forward to it, almost as a child looks forward to their birthday, as he looks forward to every weekend he has with her. It is their time together, their only time, the days of seeing her everyday another victim to Lucy's false accusations; every second weekend is, according to Lucy, more than he deserves after his bullying and controlling ways. Even talking to Jennifer has become difficult. He Skype's her everyday but most times it doesn't connect, the laptop obviously not turned on. Lucy says it is because Jennifer doesn't want to talk to him, but when he mentions it to Jennifer she says she does want to talk to him, that she misses him. Sometimes she even says she wishes that he and her mother had never broken up, and all he can say in reply is "I know," while hugging her tight, biting down on the hard and bitter need to tell her the truth of why he and Lucy are no longer together, his love for her the only thing stopping him from telling her exactly what her mother is like, knowing such information would break her heart. At the start, he would text Lucy to say he was trying to talk to Jennifer but couldn't get through, and Lucy would accuse him of being too controlling, just like in their relationship. He'd argue with her about it again and again, but she'd always end the conversation with some comment about how she refused to talk with him when he was angry, and, invariably, how his anger was further proof of his temper, and more justification for her keeping Jennifer from him, but for every second weekend.

What happens now to those weekends? What happens this weekend? What happens to their time together? Will they ever have time together again? Every day to every second weekend to… nothing?

She isn't yours.

"What..." he says, surprised that he has spoken, unsure what the rest of the sentence might be, yet aware, on some beneath-the-bone level, that if he hadn't spoken he probably would have started crying; he reckons he has cried every day since this all began, or, at the very least, every second day, huge, breath-stalling sobs that no man should ever have leave his body. He swallows, feels the aftertaste of vomit in his mouth. He thinks he might vomit again. If he does he'll do it here, onto the table, into his soon-to-be ex-wife's lap, dripping down onto the stupidly expensive handbag at her feet, the one he bought for her last Christmas, *their last* Christmas as a family.

"Who is her father?" he asks, and this time he thinks he *will* cry, because this question has come out of the same nowhere that his "what" came from, and he is even more surprised by it. He doesn't want to know that; out of all he knows and does not know, and out of all he, no doubt, is still to discover, he does not want to know that. No.

"What does it matter? Lucy says, and for a moment he feels a swell of love for her for denying him this unwanted answer, even as he realizes from her tone of voice that she deems what he has asked her as something inconsequential, or, even worse, something he has no right to know; she has said all she wishes to say and there is now an air of boredom to her, she is bored with this conversation, bored of this mediation, bored of this man who sits across from her, this man she once supposedly loved. It rolls off her in heavy waves, and he feels the pressure of it around his head, squeezing his brain.

He closes his eyes against the headache forming in his skull. He seems to be getting headaches every day of late, along with sharp, shooting pains in his jaw which he presumes are from grinding his teeth; every morning he wakes with blood in the corners on his mouth and on his pillow. Maybe when he opens his eyes again Noelle and Lucy will be gone. Or he will be gone. Maybe he'll open them and realize that he has been asleep, and these past months have been nothing but a dream, a nightmare. Maybe he is asleep right at this moment, and when he opens his eyes he will find himself lying in his bed, his wife asleep beside him, and his daughter about to jump on him, all elbows and knees and smiles as beautiful as her mother's.

She isn't yours.

He opens his eyes and sees Noelle and Lucy still sitting there, still looking at him.

"I think, unfortunately, at this juncture, it would be best for both of you to engage solicitors," Noelle says, her eyes turning from him to Lucy, and maybe it is his imagination, but her impassive expression seems to shift into hardness as she looks at Lucy, her professionalism unable to withstand the blatant cruelty on display. It is hard to be sure, with only her profile visible to him, but he can definitely see the muscles just above her jaw tightening; a flare of pain shoots along his lower cheek telling him he is tightening his own jaw, grinding his teeth. It feels good to know that some else can see it, Lucy's cruelty, her viciousness, that it is not just his imagination, or some knee-jerk, unconscious reaction to some truth he does not recognize contained within her accusations.

"I think that would be best," Lucy says, smiling at Noelle as though she is declining the offer of a cup of coffee.

It crosses Dean's mind that Lucy might be lying. She has, after all, spent years lying to him, and maintaining, with great care, those lies. What would one more lie mean? She wants to hurt him, as he, according to her accusations, has hurt her; it makes sense in that way that such senseless actions do, pain answering pain. But, it would be a cruelty beyond any human understanding, telling a father that the daughter he loves with all his being is not in fact his. Since discovering she was having an affair Dean has come to realize that his wife is not the women he believed her to be, the woman he loved deeply, the woman he married, even allowing for how a person can change over, and be changed by, the years, but if she were capable of such a devastating lie, then he never knew her at all.

Of course, if she isn't lying, and she has allowed him, over these past eight years, to believe that Jennifer was his daughter, to *raise* her as his own, then, that too proves he never had clue who she was.

She isn't yours.

No, she is not lying. He feels it deep within his body, feels its echo in the destroyed structure of his heart, the veracity of it: Jennifer is not his daughter. He has raised her, cared for her, loved her, but another man is her father. He, Dean, is nothing more than her stepfather, if even that. Does this mean that the love he feels for her will fade away? Lessen? Will he wake up tomorrow morning and not feel the pain of her absence as deeply as he does every morning she is not there? He doesn't imagine such a thing is possible. And even if it were, he doesn't know whether he would want it to happen; he doesn't want his love for her to fade away, doesn't want to lose this last decent thing in his life. Nor, in truth, does he want her absence to cease hurting, because might not that in itself be a by-product of loving her less?

She isn't yours.

Noelle is straightening her papers on the round table. Throughout this mediation she has taken notes, and he and Lucy have supplied her with various documents including their payslips, bank accounts, list of expenditures and mortgage details. She has said when the mediation is over she will return their documents to them, and shred whatever notes she has taken. There will be no record of what was said in this room, bar what they themselves remember, and judging by how Lucy seems to recall their marriage, what they remember will widely differ. Dean knows he will remember everything that was said in this room, exactly as it was said, and how he felt after each crushing word, but he would gladly forget it all, shred it all into unknowability as Noelle will shred her notes.

Lucy is rising from her chair. Before his eyes she begins to move in slow motion. Noelle too, still straightening all the documents in front of her, is now moving in slow motion. The two of them look as though they are struggling against the pull of gravity, like they are exerting unimaginable amounts of energy to make the simplest of movements. He knows he should rise from his own chair but he doesn't think himself capable of doing so, his legs, his whole body, beginning to feel like a dead weight beneath his heavy head. He doesn't *want* to move either, regardless of his ability to do so or not. He wants to remain sitting there, still, forever still, and by remaining there, somehow that will mean that Lucy will have to remain in her chair. He and his soon-to-be ex-wife will cease to move, while Noelle will continue to straighten her papers, forever tapping them on the table top.

He looks at Lucy, this woman he has loved for almost two decades, and feels the last of that love for her leak sluggishly from his body, and as it leaves him it is replaced by a pain unlike any he has ever felt before, a pain which is more like the memory of pain, or the ghost of pain, and yet is all the more debilitating for that. At the same time as he feels this, Lucy's body is released from its slow motion movements and she is already standing and pushing her chair into the table, reaching for the coat he remembers her wearing one night when he came home from a particularly hard day at work, with nothing on under it, a wicked smile shining beautifully on her face; was she having an affair then, sleeping with someone else, greeting them wearing just a coat, *this* coat? How has she done it? How? He has already wondered at great length how she was able to have so many affairs throughout their marriage and return home to him every time, kissing him, making love to him, telling him she loved him, without being able to come to any conclusion. And he knows he will reach the same nothingness as he seeks answers to how she was able to keep Jennifer's true parentage from him, and, more importantly, why she did so.

And what if he had never discovered the affair? Never confronted her about it? Would his daughter still be his daughter? Would they even be here, in this room, or would their life be continuing on as it had been? She having her affairs, and he knew the wiser. A fool in ignorance. A fool with a daughter and a wife, a family. A fool who did not know he was a fool.

He only became aware of the affair by accident, Lucy's phone beeping with a text message while it charged on his side

71

of the bed, the sockets on her side not working for some unknown reason, she in the shower after they had greeted the Saturday morning with their daughter still asleep by making slow, lazy love. He had looked at it without thinking, forgetting for a moment that it was her phone. When he realized it was hers he had already begun to read the text, his eyes continuing on to the end without any instruction from his brain, even as he felt his world crumble.

Jennifer had run in then, wide awake and ready for her cousin's birthday party, launching onto the bed, her body practically shaking with excitement. He had quickly erased the message, not thinking, and, with hands shaking, put the phone back down on his locker, before scooping Jennifer up his in arms and bringing her downstairs to give her breakfast, his hands still shaking as he poured the milk over her Coco Pops. Watching her eat her cereal and listening to her speed-talk through all she wanted to do before the birthday party, he had decided he had read the text wrong, or, at the very least, it was a fling, a moment of weakness, his wife loved him, she loved him. He didn't want to believe it. Not his wife, not his Lucy. No. She couldn't be having an affair. No, he told himself again and again, and by the time Lucy came down to the kitchen, dressed, but with her hair still wet, his hands had stopped shaking.

But he hadn't read the text wrong. Nor was it a fling. Over the following weeks, with no conscious division, he felt a shift in how he looked at his wife, a change that he somehow knew did not begin when he read that text message, but instead began when she came downstairs, her hair still wet, smiling, unaware that he had seen the text message, unaware that his heart had begun its slow breaking. He still loved her, and he told himself he still trusted her, still trying to convince himself that he'd read the text message wrong, but how he saw her became analytical, cold, and he was able to see what his love for her had prevented him from seeing: she constantly checked her phone, and would quickly look at him whenever it would beep with a text message, her whole body tightening; he never saw her phone left alone on the kitchen table or the arm of the chair, it was always with her, either out of sight in her pocket, in her bag, or in her hand; she was always distracted, lost in thought, sometimes even breaking off in mid-sentence when talking to him as though she had lost interest in the conversation. He began to question her as to why she was late home, why she never answered his calls or his texts. He commented, as casually as possible, on the fact that her phone never seemed to be out of her hand. She blamed work, demands from her boss, a new client. Sometimes she'd get angry, accuse him of not trusting her, and he would back down, bite into his retort that he had every cause not to trust her, because maybe, just maybe he was wrong, maybe he *had* read the text wrong. Maybe. Hopefully.

He couldn't sleep or eat, stress and disbelief chewing through his stomach and head. His heart. He felt like a stranger to himself, felt like he couldn't recognize the life he was living. There was a constant tight ball of tension filling his chest, and his anger never seemed to cease flaring - something that never happened - like an animal suffering from a pain it couldn't understand, snapping at people in work for the smallest of things, which earned him a stern warning from his boss, snapping at Lucy, who would snap back at him tenfold, almost snarling as she told him to leave his bad mood in work. Snapping at Jennifer.

It was this, the snapping at Jennifer, that was the last straw for him. His daughter who he never snapped at, never raised his voice to, even when she was being bold and would probably benefit from being shouted out; it was Lucy who had always been the one to shout at Jennifer, sometimes for the most simple of things. It was a simple enough thing that he had snapped at. She had left the tap running in the bathroom after brushing her teeth. He had called her back to turn it off but she said she was already in bed and about to fall asleep, using that baby voice she sometimes used when she wanted to get out of doing something. He had roared at her, his voice seeming to crack the tiles of the bathroom; he startled himself, never having heard himself make such a sound. Jennifer started crying, huge, frightened sobs, like a monster had been released into her room. Lucy had rushed upstairs to see what had happened, and ended up spending hours with her until she fell asleep, both of them refusing his repeated apologies, Lucy seeming to goad Jennifer into being stubborn. He had slept fitfully that night, and when he woke the next morning, late, his alarm not going off, even though it was set to repeat on weekday mornings - he suspected Lucy had switched it off - Lucy and Jennifer had already left the house; the bed empty beside him, the kitchen empty when he entered it, the house so silent, all of them combined to install a sense of heavy foreboding which followed him for the day.

"I know you're having an affair," he said to Lucy that night as they sat in a restaurant, just the two of them, their monthly date night, she devouring the medium-rare steak she had ordered, while his own, well-done, went cold on his plate. He had wanted to say it too her before they went out, but Lucy had to come straight from work, and he didn't want to do it over the phone, nor was there any way he would have been able to sit through the entire meal without saying something. He had considered cancelling but feared she would use that as an excuse to work late, and he could not go another night without speaking. Even as the words were shakily leaving his mouth, he was telling himself he was wrong, his stress was unfounded, his anger unnecessary. She would, rightly so, be angry that he'd accused her of something so horrible, but he would apologize, blame how busy he was in work, and she would eventually forgive him, and everything would return to normal again, before he had seen, and misread, that text message on her phone.

"Yes, I am," she had said immediately, and their marriage was over. He had looked down at his cold steak and it made his stomach turn, while adding a razored weight to his already tired body. When he looked back up at Lucy, she was cutting into her steak, watery blood leaking out of it, mixing into the oily juices of her fried onions.

The mediation had been Lucy's idea initially. She hoped they would be able to reach agreements concerning Jennifer and the house without the hassle and expense of going through the courts, and he agreed with her, telling himself that if she had this avenue to air her grievances she might see that their marriage was worth saving; he didn't want to lose her, and even though she had been unfaithful, he believed they could get beyond, *he* could get beyond it. It was in the first few minutes of their first mediation meeting that she began her decimation of their marriage, forcing huge tears from her eyes and heavy sobs from her chest as she spoke to the mediator, telling her she had been secretly seeing a therapist for months, building up her mental strength so she would have the courage to leave him. This was not the marriage he remembered. He did not recognize the man she spoke of either, one who was prone to vocal outbursts and sudden mood swings, who shook with barely contained anger, a man who needed to know where she was at every minute of every day, and refused to allow her contact with her friends. She even went as far to tell the mediator that not only was she saving herself she was saving their daughter who feared him just as much as she herself did.

He had sat there, open-mouthed, shock and a rising anger at her lies shaking his body, while any hope he harboured that they could save their marriage vanished as though it had existed nowhere but in his mind. Of all that he imagined might be said, he never once thought it would be anything like what Lucy had just said; he believed, if they did veer from the nuts and bolts of a separation, it would be in relation to her infidelity, with him, the injured and angry party, being the most vocal. When it was his turn to have his say he had denied all she had said, of course, while trying to keep the anger out of his voice, hearing it, nevertheless, sneaking into his tone with every word, which made him all the angrier, because he knew he was sounding exactly like the kind of man that Lucy had just described. When she had been telling her side to the mediator, she had looked only at Noelle, never looking at him once, though he had been staring hard at her, willing her to have the decency to at least look at him as she spun her lies. When *he* spoke, his eyes darted from Noelle to Lucy; every time he looked at Lucy she was looking at him, defiance in her eyes. Once, when he heard his voice crack with emotion, she lifted her hand to her mouth, covering, he was convinced, a smirk.

The mediation became a war, the round table they sat at the battle field. And Lucy was winning, if anyone could be considered a winner is such a vicious fight. The ambush of the first mediation meeting ceased all conversation between them, unless it was to do with Jennifer, and even then most of the communication would be through emails or texts. Sometimes, the conversations would descend into accusations and name-calling, and occasionally, Lucy would reveal another affair she had, or some one-night stand, clearly wanting to wound him even deeper, always careful to reveal them to his face, never once saying it in a text or email; at those times he felt his anger burn unhindered by the confines of the mediation room and he would say things he would later regret, horrible things to her face, and, stupidly, he knew, through texts and emails, and in the next mediation meeting, Lucy would have a print out of the conversation and use it as further proof of his temper and bullying.

That war was over now though, wasn't it? With one final, devastating blow from Lucy, it was over. There was nothing left worth fighting for.

She isn't yours.

She is at the door now, and he rises from his own chair. She looks back at him and he sees fear on her face. But it is not the same fear that was on her face when he rose quickly from the chair to rush from the room and vomit. That fear was genuine, but this fear is fake, a mask, a show, another performance for the eyes of the mediator; he cannot help but wonder why she is putting on this show, she knows as well as he does that nothing said in this room is admissible in court, and when the mediator shreds all her notes there will no proof of what was said. Is she practicing, rehearsing for when they are before a judge? He doesn't want to think about how she will act then, the performance she will put on.

"I'd prefer if you waited until I've left," she says, her voice quivering ever so slightly.

He looks at her, this stranger before him, and simply nods his head, sitting back down. He feels deflated, yet also weighed down by sadness.

His soon-to-be ex-wife opens the door but stops before she leaves the room. Speaking in a whisper so low he's not entirely sure she has said anything - she may be just sighing - she says "Sorry," and then is gone, leaving him sitting at the round table. Beside him, Noelle rises from her chair and walks across to her desk. He doesn't look at her, his eyes still on the now closed door.

He counts to twenty seconds, wondering why he picked twenty seconds and not thirty, forty, ten, then stands up; he sees himself moving in slow motion just as he saw Lucy and Noelle moving in slow motion, but he knows he is moving at a normal speed, just as Lucy and Noelle were moving at a normal speed. He remains there for a moment, as though unsure what to do next, which, when he thinks about it, isn't entirely untrue, but if he is waiting for his thoughts to arrange themselves in some sense before taking a step, he knows he will remain standing there for hours, if not days. Sighing, without looking at Noelle, or even speaking to her - which he recognizes could be construed as rudeness and further proof of Lucy's claims, but he's beyond caring about it at this stage - he walks to the door. He stands facing it for a moment; he'd like to rest his forehead against its solidness, or, possibly ram his forehead into it, but he does neither, and simply opens the door and leaves the room, pulling the door closed after him with more force than necessary, though he has done so without conscious thought. He turns the corner and walks towards the elevator just in time to see its doors slide shut, Lucy disappearing from view, her phone pressed to her ear. Without thinking about it, he rushes to the elevator and presses the call button, but it has already begun its downward journey, metal and cable thudding loudly, almost aggressively. He considers running down the two flights of stairs, beating the elevator's descent, but what would he do when he got there? What would he do as the doors opened and his soon-to-be ex-wife stepped out, probably still on her phone, talking to her lover, talking to the father of his daughter?

He doesn't know what he would do.

He doesn't move. He simply stands there, leans his head close to the elevator doors, listening to it as it descends. It would be quicker to take the stairs than wait for the elevator to reach the bottom, open its doors, let Lucy off, close its doors again and return to his floor. He is reminded of the tortoise and the hare, how it used to be Jennifer's favourite story, how they would both roar, "Slow and steady wins the race," at the end. He puts his forehead again the elevator doors, and feels, rather than hears, the elevator reach the bottom and the doors below open. He pictures Lucy stepping out and walking away, without a care in the world, on her way to their home, to their daughter. *His* daughter who isn't his daughter. His daughter who he loves. Before she was born, he had harboured doubts that he would be a good father, or to be exact, a suitable father for a girl, some fragile being he would have nothing in common with, playing with toys he had no experience of. He had wanted a boy, a sturdy boy he could teach sports to without fear of them crying simply because they fell, or were pushed over, whose toys were no different to the toys he had played with when he was a child. He had to hide his disappointment when the sonographer told them they were having a girl. But from the moment she roared out of her mother, he has loved her with a love he did not think himself capable of, a love that was so very different than the one he felt for Lucy, or for any woman he had ever loved, a love which erased all of his concerns, and, he freely admitted, made him realize how ridiculous those concerns had been. His daughter. *His* daughter.

She's isn't yours.

He lifts his head from the doors, hearing the elevator begin its return journey. Will Jennifer's love for him change when she discovers he isn't her father; he does not doubt for one moment that Lucy will tell her. She was heartbroken when he and Lucy separated, crying almost every day, before, in that way children seem skilled at, adapting to the change. Now there will be another change for her. Will her heart be broken again? Will she cry? Will she be able to adapt to it? Will she adapt as quickly as she was able to adapt to her parents no longer being together? And what if he is changed in her eyes, as she is changed in his eyes every second weekend he gets to see her: taller, older. Different. Still his daughter, but… She isn't as quick to hug him as she once was, doesn't smile as brightly seeing him, doesn't want to tell him how school is, how her friends are, what she's been up to since he last saw her. The cliché is true, they grow up fast, and maybe those changes are simply a part of that, a part of her growing up. But they grow up faster when you don't see them. And who is to say that how she is changing is not part of her growing up, but instead is a direct result of her mother pouring poison about him into her ear?

She isn't yours.

He takes two steps back from the elevator until he is back at the corner and can see the door of the mediation office. He shouldn't have let the meeting end. He shouldn't have let Lucy leave. He should have spoken up, said he wanted some clarification of what happens next. What happens this weekend that is his weekend with his daughter? What happens to all his weekends? With all that he has already missed, will he miss everything now?

She isn't yours.

He has never felt so helpless, adrift. Powerless.

She isn't yours.

He should have shouted. Roared, thumped the table, punched the wall.

She isn't yours.

How is he going to afford to pay a solicitor? The point of the mediation was to avoid as much cost as possible, only using them at the end when they reached agreements. But now? It will cost thousands. He is already paying rent for his horrible two bedroom apartment as well as still contributing to the mortgage of the house, the house which has been out of bounds to him since that first mediation meeting, Lucy claiming she feared for her safety if he was to be there, threatening him with the police if he came near. He argued against it - how could he not? - saying he would come to the house whenever he wanted, it was still his house after all, but of course she used this as more proof of his temper, even going as far to call him a bully in front of Jennifer a few days later, standing in a packed shopping centre, Lucy collecting her after his weekend. She complained that he was late, even though he wasn't, then she went on to say it was just like him, wanting to control everything, wanting everything his way, like a bully. He watched that horrible word sink deeply into Jennifer's eyes, eyes normally so very like his own, but which seemed to darken momentarily as that word took hold in her mind. She was all too aware of what a bully was, having suffered some bullying in school since the word had spread of her parent's breaking up; how she looked at him then, fleetingly as the change in her eyes was, is how he imagines she will look at him after Lucy tells her he isn't her father.

Dean remembers looking at his own father that way. Now there was an angry, bullying man, using his fists when words would not get him what he wanted, be it from his wife, his only child, or even a stranger on the street. That man better suited Lucy's description. She had never met him, but Dean had told her about him many times. He was still out there, somewhere, as far as Dean was aware. He hadn't seen him in two decades, not since his mother finally stopped fighting the cancer that was eating her alive, Dean walking away from him hours after her funeral, intent of living a life outside of his angry shadow.

Because of his father he knew the anger that gave way to violence. He could recognize it. He could tell, from looking at someone, whether they were prone to violence, whether the anger that they were clearly showing, with their shouting or shaking fists, was nothing but tension being released, or was the build up to them lashing out. It was almost like a scent they gave off, an acidic muskiness which stung the eyes and irritated the throat. He hated admitting it, and had in fact never admitted it to anyone but himself, but he could recognize it in himself, the capacity for it. He knew his anger was the anger that preceded violence. But he had a will not to be his father, not to give into the anger his father had so regularly given into; he avoided raising his voice as much as possible, and he never raised his fist to anyone, not even when he was in school and the other boys ridiculed him for his father, just as his daughter was being ridiculed for her parent's separation, his cheeks burning with shame and embarrassment, and an almost seductive sensation he could not name boiling beneath his skin, nor when he and Lucy were at a concert and he'd accidentally knocked into someone, spilling their drink, and they had replied by shouting at him and poking him in the chest with their finger, and Lucy had looked at him with something like disappointment in her eyes as he apologized and offered to buy them another drink.

There had been other times, many times, when he had wanted to punch someone, slap them. Some people needed it, deserved it. People who were asking for it with their attitudes and actions, their lies, and their betrayals. He had felt the urge to slap Lucy once or twice since she so causally admitted her affair. Not a punch, just a slap. At the very least, on their date night when she had continued eating her dinner as though nothing was amiss, he should have thrown his wine into her face. He should have done something, anything, rather than sitting there like he did, a child who'd just been disciplined. He could imagine the feeling of doing so, throwing the wine in her face, the shock that would have widened her eyes. And if he had slapped her, or if he had ever punched the many people he had encountered who deserved a punch, how glorious that sensation would be, that streak of violence finally tapped, the seductive sensation finally released? But he didn't. He never did. All they were, all they ever were, were just imaginings, thoughts, as brief and as harmless as the rush he had felt seeing Lucy's genuine fear less than thirty minutes ago. Just thoughts. Not actions. That was the difference between him and his father, who created and solved problems with his fists. That was the difference between the man he really was and the monstrous man Lucy tried to paint him as. If anyone was the monster in their marriage, it was her with her lies and affairs. Yes, she, and his father, were the monsters, unable to resist their most base instincts.

He is nothing like his soon-to-be ex-wife. He is nothing like his father.

She isn't yours.

He's not even a father...

Dean walks back to the elevator as the doors open, and, with a sigh that seems to ripple beneath his skin, he walks in.

CAMILLE ZIEGENHAGEN

Biography

Although Camille is an American citizen, Camille was born in Lausanne, Switzerland, in November of 1984. Camille first picked up writing when she was seven years old, drafting her poetry on a typewriter. She has two sisters, Nora and Libby, and is the youngest of her siblings. Her parents are Michael and Darlene. She is part of 10% of the U.S. population, which is left-handed. Camille is a 2007 graduate of Mercyhurst University. Camille is an analytical, creative, and curious individual. She strives to share writing that authentic and resonates with readers from around the globe and imparts her writing projects on Medium.com.

Camille Ziegenhagen

The Eccedentesiast

Months have come and gone;
yet no trace of you.
Distant memories become blurred dreams.
Wild thoughts run through my mind.
I can't hit the stop button.
Where have you gone?
Are you okay?
The truth aches.

Is someone listening?
Do they hear your cries?
I wonder where you are if and if you are okay.

From conversations we've had
I glean you're an eccedentesiast.
Yearning for human connection,
looking to face your pain with a strength of character and
courage.
You share your life hurts.
Hiding your fear
wishing sorrows away
You pine for simplicity's bliss.
Feeling healing from deep wounds
takes a lifetime.

We talk for hours
I wonder what thoughts rattle your beautiful mind
Where are you?

I see you question
your existential belonging in this world.

Camille Ziegenhagen

I know you unearth inner peace in
composing music the countless hours memorizing notes on the
piano.
It's a blanket of comfort shouting a beautiful thank you
quelling silent crescendos.
You share Mia & Sebastian's theme song for me upon the
piano
I'm the fortunate one who gets to listen.

I inwardly know you want someone to hear you perform.
Seeking praise and validation for your decorated talent.
It is an unforgettable piece, and you play it so well.
I hope you realize you are beyond gifted,
and if you don't, I hope someone else will.

I saw a reflection of you staring into a mirror of memories
Looking at a life filled with hope and love, with unbearable
sadness

You shared you read Sylvia Plath's first page of poetry, and
your world was forever changed.
Sylvia's poetry precariously balanced close to my window.
You share intensely deep quotes I will never forget.
I keep Percy Shelley's quote you shared close to my liver,
"No more, let life divide, what death can join together."
I ponder the depth of these words often, and perhaps you are
as well.

I share this quote with others hoping to hear perspectives I
have not heard before
These words seem to fall upon preoccupied ears
Empty stares and silence find their uncomfortable place
instead.

Camille Ziegenhagen

Delicate and intricate words become stranded passengers,
leaving behind a trail of value and meaning.

Beauty, universality, wisdom hides within the shadows of
conversations.
Teaching a genuine appreciation for layered words is rare.
Discussing the dash of life creates fear and discomfort.

Reflecting on the lessons you've taught me
after many sunsets have come and gone,
You taught me to love with all my liver
because the liver is heavier than the human heart.
And I will never forget this.

I feel you have validated me in ways no one else has.
Coupled with compliments and kindness
from your liver and heart combined,
which are refreshing and necessary in life.
You let me know my words are balming, like aloe.

I share with you we are in this so-called life together,
You tell me that you feel my support and that I don't know
how much that means to you.

Did you know you motivated me to keep writing?
You are always asking questions of others,
deflecting from your own life stories.
You are not alone.

I remind you to remember your value as a person.
Whenever you feel everything is spiraling out of control,
remember who you are and what gifts you bring to this world.
I know it is easy to forget essential life thoughts under
challenging times.

Camille Ziegenhagen

Are you're aware of your intellect and philosophical depth?

I want you to know if you're feeling
As though no one understands you
Or sees you for the incredible human you are,
And it appears your world is crashing inward.
I see you for you, and I'll catch you if you fall.
I hope one day soon you see it too.
Or perhaps Sylvia Plath's line of poetry will remind you to
keep on going.
There is a cleared pathway waiting for you.

I hear the intricate and thoughtful curated details you note,
which may be left unseen by others.
I've met no one else like you.
Inquisitive, emotionally intelligent, aware, astute
an empath, a connoisseur of words, a giver in life
puzzling and intriguing
like a twelve-hundred page novel from your favorite local
bookstore
wanting someone to solve
The equation of you.
Have I missed any other characteristics of you?

Staying at a distance,
yet close enough to let in
bits and pieces of who you are
I hope your parents are proud
of the person, you've grown up to be.
I hope your sister lets you vent to her,
As a shoulder to lean on.
Allowing you to find validation
from those you open yourself up to
who reminds you that everything will be okay.

Camille Ziegenhagen

We had a late-night life chat one evening;
about the ocean of existence
when neither of us could sleep
staying up in anticipation
to have an intense life conversation
With a like-minded person
is rare, refreshing and intimate these days.

We talked for five hours,
we could hardly believe it.
You let in the conversation, "While we are alive, let's be alive.
"

It is a simple statement but filled with complexities,
peeled back onions only understand.
I feel I have had some of the best and meaningful
conversations
between the seconds and minutes of these hours.
Human connection is magical.
Yet, at times, maybe, temporary.
I accept it for its derived value.

Nestled on the floor,
My head lays resting against a throw pillow,
With my eyes half-closed,
On the cusp of a dreamlike state,

Your appetite hides your inner self from relishing life.
A pale reflection appears on the screen in front of me,
I tell you I'm worried,
but the pain you carry evaporates
off the deep waters of inner realization,
like a cup of cold water thrown onto hot coals.

Camille Ziegenhagen

I listen intensely to your curtly guided questions about my
path
I respond with early morning curated thoughts
To nudge awake your internal wounds

We share our dreams,
You grace me with compliments
Affirming my honesty and transparency
You'd like to emulate both.
Kindly tell me what a wonderful,
magnetic human being I am
You graciously thank me for my authenticity.
You say there should be more of me in the world.

I struggle to accept your compliments,
inside my heart hides to tell you
"Thank you a thousand times over."
But for others your selfless words
Cease to go
unnoticed.

We agree
validation, approval, and pride
are bemusing feelings inked from other thoughtless voices
hopelessly wanting our link pads stamped
to Stain
to Mask
to Smear
one's hidden Essence

We discuss troubles people we know and not know
and people we once knew who passed away so early in this
fleeting consciousness of being human.   (I want to cut some of
the unnecessary words here)

Camille Ziegenhagen

You tell me,
"People's untimely deaths are a reminder to
love loudly in our lives and
love each other loudly while we can,
nothing in life is promised,
especially not tomorrow.

I wanted to talk to you about what keeps you awake at night.
Instead, you changed the future by doing what you do in a
moment's notice.
Shying away from talking about yourself.
Packaging the intense emotions you may feel each day.
Boxes don't always stay closed.
I can only hope you have left you're safe halfway open.
Unlocking all your troubles and worries.
Gently reminding yourself, it's okay not to be okay.
You tell me you feel my support
Unknowing how much this rope line means to you.
I hope you find someone you trust to share your pain.
Someone who will help your carry-on, weigh less.
Teaching you to let go, to let love in, and to believe in yourself.

Connecting with others in this vast world
Strengthens my empathy
and ability to self-reflect by tenfold
eventually growing from painful life realities
to a bright, yellow sunflower in an open field,

I remind you to be kind and take care of yourself
And to be clear from harm's way, safe.
self-compassion is a magnificent experience.
Before we sign off, you tell me to "Dream beautiful things."

Camille Ziegenhagen

Time never ceases
It's been over four months,
and your presence is missing.
I'm worried about you.
You told me you're disappearing
from the grid
and you will reach out when you're ready
After your voyage of self-exploration.
You reassure me
In the end, you will be okay.

How do I know with perfect certainty your heart is still strong
and beating rhythmically?
How do I know you are still sharing profound quotes and
asking others insightful questions?

I remain feeling uncertain about your state of mind.
Your last text sent says, "Please pray for me."

I wish to be more present for you.
I want you to know I see you and I hear you.

When my constant worried
and anxious thoughts hit pause
you send me a sign
you feel more centered
yet you're a continuous work in progress;
I'll know for certain
Traces of you
aren't far away.

Your sheer presence is wandering through a book aisle nearby.
Time waits for no one.
Lost in your mind and soul,

discussing your impressions of your favorite book or an intense
quote which enchants you.
And painting mysterious art candy on bathroom walls.

We are all part of life chaos together
Driving down every one-way street returning to where you
once began,
never finding an exit.

You have much to offer
You need the world,
and the world needs you.
When you feel more centered
Please send me a glow in the star-filled night sky
so I'll know for certain
you are finding your way back to the grid of life.

Camille Ziegenhagen

A Global Friendship

You are a bright, yellow rose.
You can make me
laugh and smile, at
everything, anything,
and nothing at all.
Even if tears trickle down the
middle of my cheeks,
You can spark joy in corners of
conversations.
You are a ray of light.
Streaming in at the end of a day.
You are my 8:00 PM today;
I'm you're 1:00 AM tomorrow.
A five-hour gap wedged in between these times,
The conversations are consistent and meaningful.
Impenetrable silence sequestered in the middle
Of spoken words,
Rarely meets loneliness.
Talking about our various cultures,
Life's array of hills and valleys,
What fills each of our days.
Inquiring what the other is thinking,
Even if it isn't easy to share the things that scare you the
most.
Sharing live protesting with me that that took place only a
few feet away.
Women and men alike are objecting loudly in the middle
of the street,
Late into the last hours of the night,
Feeling frustrated and angry, misled and hopeless,
Present to support their own thoughts and ideologies;
Dreaming about future possibilities in their lives.
Possibly pondering what life would be like if immigration is
an option.
Or wondering if staying in the same country,
Would improve or continue to decline.

Camille Ziegenhagen

You share an expression with me that I taught you some time ago.

I did so to teach a lesson on the importance of acceptance.

I have to practice this often, as words are easier said than done.

It's unfortunate circumstances, but as you say, "It is what it is."

Letting me know you're not a part, but solely an observer.
Talking about one's own country's political state of being
Can be fear-inducing and stressful to discuss
So much so, you don't want to speak about it
It is actually heartbreaking.
Please be safe.
You keenly know that your government needs reform.
You want what's best for everyone,
You have a natural love for your country.
Fighting for your national flag whenever you can.
You're ready for a positive change in politics.
As it would make all the difference.
Please be safe.
Around the corner and down two blocks

Your favorite tea shop where all the locals go to solely be is loud, yet comfortable to you.

Sipping steaming hot tea, catching up with a friend, and playing checkers.

Perhaps it's a place of warmth and a stop for a meeting of the minds.

Each person deserves to be seen and heard, even if you take a stance.

When it seems like no one listens and no one cares,
Write and write well.
Weigh your options.

Do something that will forever change your life for the greater good.

Listen to your heart.
Remember to be safe.
Your pursuit of happiness is a work in progress.
Stay in your home country and open a shop.

Move to France, land a job, speak French, and eat fresh-baked croissants forever.

Win the Green Card Lottery and make your mark in the States, mapping out your own kind of dream.

I wonder what your future holds.

Whatever you decide,

Always be safe.

I can't say I know for sure what it's like in your homeland.

But I can empathize with the intrinsic details you've shared.

And the different stories I've read.

It's a harsh world out there, I know.

Despite everything that surrounds you,

You're cool and collective.

With a sense of humor and smarts.

I've never seen or heard you become moody, upset, or mad.

Even though I know you are,

Maybe it's part of your native culture when you do.

Or sometimes things go unsaid that get under your skin.

Which may be overwhelming and hard to face?

Doing your best to keep them simmering.

I know one day you will face these things.

And overcome obstacles you never thought you could.

I know some topics that make you bent of shape.

It's not fair, I get it.

I've heard it said that anger is an outward expression

Of hurt, fear, and frustration.

What are you afraid of?

If I were in similar-sized shoes, my heart would ache,

And my blood would boil, hoping upon hope.

For opportunities for a better tomorrow in a broken country

Or in a different place, where fear has lessened and dreams come true.

Kindness is in your nature,

Even if a storm rumbles through,

You seem to find the silver lining in the gray sky above.

You have thoughts and opinions.

And you are true to them to the core.
You are always on the edge of your seat.
You've heard, "Patience is a virtue."
But it's the last thing on your mind.
As you can barely sleep without,
Knowing what's coming next.
You are your own kind of awesome.
You don't even have to try.
You are you.
That's what matters the most.
Talking for twenty minutes or two hours
I don't keep track.
Speaking in conversational French,
You are quick to tell me, "I hate French. Don't speak in
French. Speak in English, please."
It's fascinating and amusing to speak in another language.
I reluctantly switched to English, but not for long.
I toss Arabic words into the conversation, recognizing my
third generation roots that lie along the blue
Mediterranean.
Familiarity evokes comfort or breeds contempt.
My Arabic is far from fluent.
It's acceptable to you, as it is your own native language.
English is your second language of preference.
As you studied linguistics at the university.
Sometimes, I think your English is better than mine.
However, it is still a work in progress.
The countless times you've used the word, really.
It's comical in different ways.
I know you know this.
Do you love saying this six-letter word?
Do you use it when you are unsure of what to say?
Or is it solely for effect?
I haven't figured it out yet, and I am curious to know the
answer.
You ask, "Are you tired?"
It's late for you, 2:00 AM to be fair.
Hinting sleep is soon,
Avoiding becoming a zombie the following day,

It's inevitable.

Those two powerful words are quickly said before the call ends.

"Be safe."

Are you telling me to take care of myself, or is it discreetly about your own safety?

You may get me,
In a way, few people do.
Seeing my true colors for what they are
And nothing more.
I'm so glad we crossed paths.
Thank you for-
The endless life chats,
On any given day,
Listening and understanding
Learning about the thoughts and opinions of another person
Laughter and smiles,
Perspectives and insights I never knew before
And for this global friendship.
Please be safe.

EDUARD SCHMIDT-ZORNER

Biography

Eduard Schmidt-Zorner is a translator and writer of poetry, haibun, haiku and short stories.

He writes in four languages: English, French, Spanish and German and holds workshops on Japanese and Chinese style poetry and prose.

Member of four writer groups in Ireland and lives in County Kerry, Ireland, for more than 25 years and is a proud Irish citizen, born in Germany.

Published in 79 anthologies, literary journals and broadsheets in USA, UK, Ireland, Japan, Sweden, Italy, Bangladesh, India, France, Mauritius, Nigeria and Canada.

Writes also under his pen name: Eadbhard McGowan

Eduard Schmidt-Zorner

Life, A Timeless Theatre

The day was drawing to a close and the street lighting was coming on. When I left the train at the Metro station *Strasbourg Saint-Denis*, it was time for the evening aperitif. I went across over the road for a glass of *Pastis* into a small bistro on the corner *Rue Blondel*.

On my way, I crossed the *Boulevard de Bonne Nouvelle*, where the luminous letters of a corporate advertisement flashed through the night, extinguished, lit up, extinguished again: the first name flashed, then it remained dark for a few seconds, whereupon the company or brand name appeared in bright red. Then everything went black. After a short stop, the electric mechanism spelled the name. A green letter, a yellow one, etc. The cars that headed towards *Gare de l'Est* or *Châtelet* took a fragment of the name with them on the body of their cars.

Yellow light came from a shop window at the right-hand side of the bistro that I was approaching. On an enamel sign, which had once been blue, the words: *Montaleau-Purchase and Sales,* were written in gold letters. This was a pawnshop about to close. A man came out, holding a rod with a hook in his hand. With this, he pulled the iron security grid down. He looked at the night sky as if trying to reconcile his own meteorological observations with the weather forecast. In front of a restaurant two houses down the road, a waitress placed chairs on marble tables.

On the other side of the bistro a building with a horizontal black marble board, engraved on it in silver letters: *Fabrics F. Halimi, dress fabric, woolen, cotton and silk fabric, wholesale and retail.*

I entered the bistro. There was no longer the hustle and bustle of what happened here in the past: a meeting place of actors and theatre people without jobs, or those associated with actors and the theatre scene. Extras, minor theatre actors, musicians of all genres. Here at the round tables the contracts were negotiated but hardly anything was consumed in the bistro. They were sitting for hours in front of a cold coffee and waited to be discovered by an agent and to get a small role in some unimportant theatre in the province or in a theater play for a charity event. Until the bistro owner one day loudly exclaimed: "Excuse me, Mesdames, Messieurs, but we are not a theatre agency here."

Frédéric Laffère greeted me as he approached the counter. He was sitting there with a sincere looking couple, apparently from the stage performance scene. Frédéric is a freelance agent, who, tireless, is constantly looking for talents.

"A Kir Royal, a Perrier and a glass of Sancerre for us, quickly please."

The owner went deliberately slowly behind the counter and reached for the bottle with the *cassis*, filled the glasses, and brought them to the table in the recess.

"Here we are," he said, putting the drinks on the table, "A Perrier, a Sancerre, and a Kir Royal."

Marcel Bleu, a writer, who put away his pen a while ago after publishing five books with esoteric content and who had had remarkable success, paid for his coffee and croissant and passed the three at the neighbouring table.

"Bonsoir, Edouard, ça va? Are you still involved in poetry? I saw your article about French poetry in *Le Point*. Well done. Why are you writing poems? " he asked.

"I don't know, " I said. "Maybe words have to find their way out of my mind, pour out, and I try to collect them and put them into rhymes"

With a trembling hand, he pulled a picture postcard out of his jacket pocket and said, "Look here, a picture postcard. They have become rare. When did you get a picture postcard last? I like a hand-written card or letter; it is something intimate and personal. I even started to write and send Christmas cards again to my friends. You cannot put the computer screen on the mantel piece, but cards give it a totally different appearance. As if friends wave over to you. I got four cards in return. People are taking photos with their digitals and are sending them with messages to their friends in all the networks. However, I cherish those old relics. Do you know, who sent me the card? ... *Amélie*, you know, the actress, who was famous in the 1970s and ended in *Folies Bergère*. She lives now in Deauville and is married to a boring, ugly, old but rich man. But I still get a greeting from time to time. We were lovers a long time ago. "He sent a dreaming look to the ceiling. Then he winced as if awakening from a dream.

"And here." He pulled a bulky camera out of his bag. "A *Voigtländer*. Most of the young people perhaps never heard this name. I found it in the attic. It belonged to my mother. It was an adventure though to find a shop, which is still selling films for this antique. I like photos; they have something eternal, although morbid as well.

Provokingly I am raising attention in public, when I take photos and feel that the people are whispering behind my back, when I am bustling about with this old-fashioned camera. I see it in their looks: 'The old chucklehead with his old scrap camera.' I am now looking for a tripod to make it even more dramatic or a camera with this black cloth, which the photographers of old pulled over their heads. I would stand in front of *Notre Dame* on a Sunday and shout at the church goers, 'Say Cheeeeese.'"

I replied, "Nothing new. Nothing changed dramatically in life. Theatre and fashion are good examples. Fashion never changed really, well yes, the colours, the sizes, the fabric, the width of the lapels, wider, narrower, the cut of the trousers, with creases or without, there is nothing really new since Prussian times. Men still wear the uniform jackets, which the Prussian officers were wearing in the seventeenth century. Same applies to the stage. The stage design might change from traditional design to ultramodern, with more light effects, provocations, technical innovations but the performing actor or actress are still performing since times immemorial. Not even this bistro has changed in the last 30 years nor have the guests. "

Marcel Bleu nodded his head. "Did you read my book which was published recently?"

"Yes, I bought it in *Rue Cadet*. I read the first chapter. "

"For the Templars, Baphomet was the key to everything and thus a symbol for the result of a formal process: the accomplished initiation. That is what I remembered from the cover text. A lot of research went into it, I presume. "

"Yes, "he said. "It took me five years. I travelled to most of the Templar sites in France, Italy and Germany. "

"But you got behind the secret"?

"There are no secrets, only explanations and emotions. All those, who claim or pretend to have the 'great secret' have a hand full of sand. It is like letting sand run through the fingers on a stormy day at the beach, grains of sand gone and taken by the wind.

The bistro owner came over to us. "Can I serve you something? I have still fresh quiche with mushrooms and leek".

Bleu sat down at the table, I joined him.

"Ok, I was about to leave and had paid, but let us sit down and have this delicious quiche. And, yes, I take a glass of your Bordeaux."

"Same for me please," I added.

One could hear the tick-tock of the pendulum clock.

I looked out of the window.

Suddenly two cars nearly collided, brakes squealed and made a hair-raising sound. Angry voices could be heard. Then the road returned to a churchyard silence. The wet pavement glistened bleakly under the shine of the street lanterns, like blind mirrors.

The quiche was served. The fine smell tickled the nose. The owner poured a glass of wine. Bleu tasted the wine and approved it. My glass was filled.

"We should find a new way to get people interested in poetry." Bleu started to rekindle the conversation again.

We heard cheers from the table, where Frédéric was in conversation with the couple. Apparently, they had come to an agreement.

We exchanged a few more words. Bleu developed his idea of an innovative publishing house for emerging poets, reflecting the many languages which were spoken in France. We spoke about a book, which a mutual friend launched in Amiens last month. Then the conversation stalled, fell practically asleep. I let it rest. Bleu was already overwhelmed by fatigue, sated by the quiche and the wine and finally he closed his eyes.

An end of a late evening, wrapped in a Parisian night in a bistro near *Boulevard de Bonne Nouvelle* reveals that nothing has changed in life; the old comedy is still going on, only the actors change.

CHRISTINE HENNEBURY

Biography

Whether she is telling them aloud or in writing, writer/storyteller Christine Hennebury favours stories that unfold in unexpected ways. More of her flash fiction can be found on her website ChristineHennebury.com and in her self-published collection *Disconcerted*.

Christine Hennebury

Handkerchiefs

The notebook was obviously supposed to be a secret.

That must be why Alan kept it at the bottom of the drawer, right in the back, under his handkerchiefs, of all things. He never used handkerchiefs at all, so they had made a good hiding place.

Josie had asked him about them once, the handkerchiefs, when they were both putting laundry away. It had been a nice, ordinary, couple moment. Each of them taking their own laundry out of the same basket then tucking it away in drawers.

It was the kind of moment that, if they were in a movie, they would have chosen to have a deep, soul-searching, relationship-shaping talk.

But they weren't in the movies. They weren't having a big talk. They were having a little talk.

It was about ordinary things...where he had gotten that shirt, who gave her that necklace, why the little clay change dish on his dresser was lopsided (his niece had made it in pottery class when she was five).

The handkerchiefs were just one part of that easy, rolling chat about nothing.

His Mom gave him handkerchiefs with his birthday present every year. She said that a gentleman always carried a handkerchief. Once, when he was young, he mentioned that his father never carried them and his Mom had replied, "Exactly."

They had both laughed about that at the time. It was ridiculous to think of his mother being happily married to someone that she didn't want her son to take after. Josie asked if his mother had ever said anything about it to his Dad, but Alan figured that his mother had just kept it to herself.

The whole conversation had happened months ago, but Josie often rolled it around in her mind.

How could someone carry a small secret resentment like that and never say anything about it, never give the other person a chance to change?

How could Alan's mother keep quiet about it? How could his father not know?

Josie was putting their laundry away alone today. There was no crisis, no rift, he was washing the dishes, so she had come upstairs with the basket.

Putting his socks in the drawer, her hand had nudged the handkerchiefs and brushed against the coil of the notebook hidden beneath them. She knew better, but she couldn't stop herself from having a peek.

Alan kept a list of every single thing she did that got on his nerves. They were small things, leaving hair clips on the table, rolling her socks into balls, leaving the spoon and tea bag balanced on the corner of the sink. The secret list was long, pages and pages of annoyances recorded and then, apparently, dismissed.

She closed the notebook, placed her palm on the cover, and took a deep breath.

Clearly, Alan took after his mother.

Perhaps Josie could, too.

With a quick nod, she tucked the notebook back under the handkerchiefs, and turned to put the rest of their laundry away.

DANNY BARBARE

Biography

Danny P. Barbare resides in the Upstate of the Carolinas. He attended Greenville Technical College, where his poetry won the Jim Gitting's Award and his poetry has been nominated for Best of Net by Assisi Online Journal. He lives with his wife and family and small sweet dog Miley. He enjoys traveling locally, especially to Carl Sandburg's old house in Flat Rock, NC.

Good Days!

It
Is
Simply
This

I'm
Happy
To
Be
Headed
Home

As
The
Days
Are
Growing
Warmer
And
Longer

And
I
Can't
Wait
To
See
You.

A Janitor's Letter

Says the
Janitor

Where
Would
We
Be
Without
One
Or
The
Other

We
Would
Be
Incomplete

Like
A
Dustpan
And
Broom

The
Floor
Wouldn't
Be
Clean.

Growing Up!

I
Have
Manners
At
The
Maple
Table

May
I
Have
The
Bowl

After
The
Prayer

I
Eat
With
My
Mouth
Closed

I
Am
Quiet.

DC DIAMONDOPOLOUS

Biography

DC Diamondopolous is an award-winning novelette, short story, and flash fiction writer with over 200 stories published internationally in print and online magazines, literary journals, and anthologies. DC's stories have appeared in: *34th Parallel, So It Goes: The Literary Journal of the Kurt Vonnegut Museum and Library, Lunch Ticket, Raven Chronicles, Silver Pen, Blue Lake Review,* and many others. DC was nominated for Best of the Net Anthology. She lives on the California central coast with her wife and animals. dcdiamondopolous.com

Blonde Noir

Kit Covington sat on the sofa in her Pacific Palisades mansion with a cigarette lodged in the side of her mouth. A cloud of smoke floated around her head. She adjusted the oxygen tube in her nose, then brushed ash from her dog Muffin's champagne-colored curls. The miniature poodle dozing in Kit's lap startled when the camera crew from The Great Morning Talk Show banged equipment into Kit's antique furniture.

"Watch it! You scratch anything, you'll pay for the restoration." Since her left lung had been removed, Kit's husky voice had a rattle that lingered between words chaining them together like loose ball bearings.

"Sorry," the stocky, tattooed sound woman said.

Kit wondered if the all-female crew was a set-up—some kind of knife-twisting in the gut. She'd been anxious about the interview and now regretted it.

Her son, Robin, urged her to confront the nonsense. The 1950s blonde bombshell became notorious because of some damn YouTube video a pop singer made by superimposing Kit's dance sequence from the 1956 movie, *I Was a Teenage SheWolf From Mars*, while he sang to her. It went viral. Paramount capitalized on it with a box set of her films. The Screen Actors Guild sent her checks she hadn't seen in sixty years.

Kit would have laughed at the male juvenile obsession with her big breasts, platinum blonde hair, and erotic gyrations in her bullet bra and tight sequined space suit. But it happened at the time actresses came forward and named producers, directors, and actors who raped and assaulted them. The video ignited a firestorm of criticism from young women, who blamed her for their being sexualized. She became the poster girl, Adam's Eve, the anti-feminist, the target for all the ills cast upon womanhood—making her name Kit into a verb synonymous with "fucks for favors."

What a load of shit!

Kit had had enough after months of headlines, CNN pestering her old studio for her telephone number, and the tabloids offering money to anyone who had a recent picture of her.

Centerfolds, headshots, movie-posters, her sexy blonde images from the 50s were everywhere.

She chose The Great Morning Talk Show because Bridget Lundgren, the lawyer turned TV host, defended her on the show.

Muffin jumped from Kit's lap and wolfed a piece of jelly donut the beefy, spiked-haired, lighting woman had dropped.

"This isn't a barn! Use a napkin. That's a three-hundred-year-old Persian rug," Kit said.

"Sorry, Miss Covington."

Kit watched Lundgren scrutinize the pictures on the wall. She was a real fashion plate in a navy pantsuit, with her short blonde hair tucked behind her ears. Kit tensed when the woman took a photograph from her carnival days off the wall and examined it, revealing a yellow nicotine outline. How dare she!

"Is this from the Gerling Carnival?" Lundgren asked.

"Could be," Kit said surprised that Lundgren knew about her carny days.

Lundgren replaced it and moved to the photo of Kit riding bareback in The Barnum and Bailey Greatest Show on Earth, where she performed flips until she fell from the horse and broke her ankle.

Above the walk-in fireplace, Lundgren gazed at the huge painting of Kit by Willem de Kooning. It was Kit's favorite, by the artist who inspired her to take up painting. Completed in 1958 when she was twenty-five, the painting recalled the memory of sitting for hours, her back arched, her tits pointing to the North Star, pouty full lips, a halo of platinum blonde hair, and the moist come-hither look women still use to lure men into the bedroom.

"This is one of the few de Koonings I've seen that isn't an abstract," Lundgren said. "He did others."

"My favorite was the Woman series. I love how he broke rules."

Kit puffed on her cigarette and flicked ash into a large serving dish sitting next to her. She wondered how much of the art world Lundgren knew. In person, Kit judged her as a cool and calculating woman, the way she inspected the pictures as if they hid the da Vinci code. Why not ask how all the hullabaloo affected her, how it made her irritable, critical, bitchy. She wondered if Lundgren had gone so far as to play nice-nice on TV— knowing Kit would be watching.

Outside the sliding screen door, she saw Robin watering the rose bushes. Since the operation, he'd been pestering her to stop smoking. She cut back from a four packs a day, to two and a half. What the hell did he want? She'd been smoking since she was ten. When he tried to scare her with images on his phone of how the cancer could spread to the liver and kidneys, she grabbed the phone and threw it at him. She made him swear that when she died, he'd put her in a box, stick a cigarette in her mouth—preferably lit— and prod a lighter in her right hand.

"I can go without oxygen for four minutes," Kit said. "So, break. I don't want these damn tubes on camera. I'll need a cigarette—"

"Your son told us."

Miffed by Lundgren's rudeness, Kit said, "When do we start?" "In five minutes. Do you need to use the restroom?"

"My legs are cramping." Kit struggled to rise, shooing Lundgren away when she tried to help. She stood and rolled the oxygen tank she called Sherman across the living room floor while pulling a pack of Winstons and a lighter from the pocket of her long flowing gypsy skirt.

"Aren't you afraid of the tank exploding?" the sound woman asked as Kit wobbled by.

"No, I'm not. If I could walk a tightrope while on my period, I can roll a damn dolly while smoking a ciggie."

The girl raised her eyebrows and turned away.

Robin saw her and slid open the screen.

"I don't want to do this," Kit said. "That woman's going to ambush me."

"C'mon mom, you liked her."

"Not anymore. She snapped at me, 'Your son told us,'" she mimicked.

Kit pushed past Robin and stood above her tiered English garden. Even with her fading sense of smell, she caught fragrances of her lemon and peach trees. Below the garden was a view overlooking Highway 1, Malibu, and the Pacific Ocean. She had bought the house in the fifties while pregnant with Robin and married his father Daniel soon after.

The April morning glistened as Catalina Island sat like a treasured cast-off from the mainland. Cast-off. When Kit hit her late twenties, it was over. No producer wanted to hire an old hag at thirty. Her agent got her jobs on TV, as a panel member on To Tell the Truth, I've Got a Secret, and her big whoop-de-doo, the center box on Hollywood Squares. In the 1970s, her agent dropped her.

"You signed a contract, Mom. Let people hear your story." He peered into the living room. "They're ready for your close-up."

Kit rolled her eyes. Robin was always quoting from *Sunset Blvd.*, *The Wizard of Oz*, or *All About Eve*. On occasion, he'd dress in drag and perform dance numbers from *Cabaret*, *A*

Chorus Line, and musicals she never heard of. Her boy knew how to make her laugh.

Kit counted five strangers in her house, eating, drinking coffee, moving her furniture, and using her bathroom. Well, at least they were women and wouldn't be pissing on the floor.

"We're ready, Miss Covington," the sound woman yelled.

"C'mon, Mom. It'll be fun."

"I look like an old beatnik."

"You are an old beatnik."

Kit's chuckle rumbled like a truck bouncing over potholes. She smoothed her long white hair with her ciggie hand. She hadn't worn lipstick or make-up in years. She lived in sandals and, before the operation, went barefoot.

Robin waited for Kit to enter, then slid the door behind him. Kit rolled Sherman to the couch and settled in. Muffin jumped in her lap and Jezebel the cat slinked around the sofa and nestled beside Kit.

"We'll open with the video," Lundgren said. "Then cutaway for the interview."

"Why show that again?"

"It's the reason for the interview, Miss Covington."

How sucky, Kit thought. She wasn't ashamed. She just didn't like having to defend herself.

"Everyone in the world has seen it."

"It's a lead in," Lundgren said.

Kit scowled at Robin. He came over and straightened the string of turquoise and silver beads that dangled from her neck.

"Quit fussing."

"Come out, come out, wherever you are and meet the young lady who fell from a star," Robin whispered.

"Glinda the Good Witch," Kit mumbled.

Robin winked at her.

"Ready when you are, Bridget," the camerawoman said.

"Good morning. Today, we have a very special guest. Kit Covington. In case you've been living under a rock the last several months," Lundgren smiled, "we're going to play the video that's caused a sensation. Here's the Grammy-winning pop star, Walker, singing from the hit video, "You're My Dream Girl in the Night" along with Kit Covington from her movie, *I Was a Teenage SheWolf from Mars*."

The video played on a small monitor. Kit watched herself from the 1956 horror movie, dancing, spinning, cleavage bouncing, her generous ass stretching the satin on her sequined spacesuit. It was hard to imagine her wrinkled and shriveled body once had so much oomph and had been so sexy.

She took off the tube and laid it beside her.

The camerawoman pointed her finger, and Lundgren began.

"We're sitting in the home of Kit Covington, a movie actress known as the Queen of the Bs from the 1950s, who has become infamous for being the poster-girl for the sexualization of generations of women."

"That's a load of shit!" Kit said. "Why blame me? Women have always used their bodies to get what they want. As if women didn't fuck before 1956."

Lundgren's jaw dropped. Seconds went by before she made the throat-slash sign with her hand.

Kit coughed and hacked. Muffin jumped on the floor. Jezebel leaped from the sofa and ran around the couch. Kit took the tube and fastened the nasal cannula inside her nostrils, then lighted up a Winston. She inhaled and glanced at the stunned crew and Lundgren. Robin, with his eyes popping and mouth opened, reminded her of Joan Crawford in *Whatever Happened to Baby Jane*.

"You can't swear on TV," Lundgren said.

Kit glanced at her, looked away, and flicked ash into the dish. It was a knee-jerk reaction, a build-up from the last several months. Also, she wasn't convinced Lundgren was on her side.

"You can't go off the rails like that, Miss Covington. It won't help you."

"Infamous. Sexualization. Men sexualize women. Who's head of advertising? They use sex to sell hamburgers, anything. Look at films! Who runs the networks?"

"It's a lead-in," Lundgren said.

"I've been assaulted and harassed like all those women. I don't blame anyone but the shits who hurt me." Kit blew smoke at the side of Lundgren's face. "How dare you judge me."

Lundgren waved away the smoke. "I'm not, Miss Covington. Not at all." Jezebel arched her back and rubbed against Lundgren's leg.

Kit crushed the cigarette into the plate. She narrowed her gaze at the blonde, who with her furrowed brow and the gentle way she stroked and caressed Jezebel, didn't fool Kit. Behind Lundgren's look of compassion was a frozen dish of ambition.

"Would you like to try it again?" Lundgren said.

Kit caught the rapport— the way Lundgren and Robin shot glances at each other— and now her cat had turned traitor.

She took off the oxygen tube. "Muffin." The poodle ran to her and leaped in her lap.

Robin sat at the far end of the couch.

"We're ready," the camerawoman said.

Lundgren looked into the camera.

"We're here with Kit Covington. Known in the 1950s as Queen of the Bs, she has made a scandalizing comeback—"

115

"Scandalizing! That's nothing compared to the shit I see on HBO." Lundgren made the throat-slash sign and stood from the sofa. "We need to take a break."

"We sure as hell do." Kit attached the oxygen tube and rose from the couch. Muffin bounded to the floor. Kit wheeled Sherman to the screen door, shooing Robin away, opened it, and went outside.

"Mom?"

Kit ignored him. She wheeled Sherman down the ramp while lighting a cigarette.

She and her boy had been snookered into believing Lundgren was on her side. "Scandalizing," she mumbled. What did Lundgren know about the life of a girl in the 1940s? Those young punks don't know a damn thing about what life was like before they were born.

She clamped the ciggie in the corner of her mouth and steered the wheels over the yellow bricks Robin had laid that led down to her studio. She'd shut the door, pick up her pallet and brush, and lose herself as she disappeared into her painting.

The white stucco building, with red bougainvillea blooming against the side of the wall, inspired the artist in Kit. She painted color in splashes and dashes, mix-matching paint, blending oil, watercolor, and charcoal onto the canvases. Entering her studio was the closest thing to going to church. It was a place where her creativity transported and elated her.

She mashed the cigarette into the standing ashtray outside. The galleries complained of having to clean her canvases. To show her how the smoke diminished her work, Robin took a moist cloth and gently wiped a painting. The rag turned yellow. Without the cover of nicotine, the colors burst with vitality. It was a huge sacrifice not to smoke while she painted, but for her art, she would do anything.

Kit went into her sanctuary, the studio overlooking her cactus garden. Rows of tall windows allowed light to stream in. And where there weren't windows, her imagination decorated the walls. Robin had constructed built-ins for stacking paintings, nooks for brushes and paints, a worktable with drawers. Her boy built the studio exactly how she insisted.

In the late 1980s, Robin went behind her back and entered her work in contests. Furious by Robin's betrayal, even when she won, she wouldn't talk to him for days. He adored being the son of a movie star but being her art agent satisfied both his nurturing and dramatic nature. He arranged her exhibits at MoMA, the Whitney, and others, with as much flare as his once movie star mother. He made deals so her work hung in The Metropolitan Museum of Art and the Prado.

From the beginning she signed her work D. L. Hawkins, after Robin's father, leaving off his last name, Sutton. He lived his forty-four years as an art form, free and spontaneous, he danced when other men walked. My God how she missed him.

Kit made a fortune from her paintings, donating millions of dollars to art institutes. Who would take her seriously if they knew the esteemed D. L. Hawkins was once a second-rate sex-kitten?

Kit shut the door against the world. It hurt having those young women wrongly judge her. She knew what women went through, especially young women. Mad at herself for being so sensitive, she hated to admit that she cared what others thought of her.

"I knocked, but you didn't answer."

Kit turned so fast the oxygen cannula pulled at her nostrils.

The blonde talk show host stood in the doorway, holding Muffin. Lundgren wore the same expression—open mouth, wide eyes—as when Kit dropped the f-bomb.

"Oh my God. I don't believe it."

"I'm not doing the interview," Kit said.

Lundgren gazed at the art on the walls. "Neither am I, Miss Covington."

"Then why are you here? And why are you holding my dog?"

"I followed Muffin," Lundgren said, releasing the poodle. "She brought me here."

"Fink," Kit said, glaring at the dog.

"I wanted to let you know I cancelled." Lundgren continued to stare at the art and the unfinished oil painting on the easel. "And to say goodbye." Lundgren shook her head. "I can't believe it," she said, looking at a pastel that leaned against the wall. "I'm standing in D.L. Hawkins's studio."

Kit hacked, "Th—This is," she stuttered, "private."

"I'm sorry. I swear—swear, I won't mention a word to anyone. Are you and Hawkins an item?" she said, glancing at Muffin's bed and water dish in the corner.

Shaking, startled by the intrusion into her secret life, Kit watched dumbfounded as Lundgren made a b-line to the easel.

"You, you're not supposed—" Kit stammered.

"A merry-go-round, where the horses are riding the people."

Didn't Lundgren hear her? Just barged her way into D. L.'s studio as if Kit didn't exist. She shuffled across the wooden floor, shoving Sherman over to the easel.

Lundgren angled her head. "Animal cruelty. It's amazing to me how Hawkins takes an idea and turns it on its head. I saw his exhibit at MoMA when I did my post-graduate work. Blew me away."

"You know his work?"

"I majored in art. Didn't have the talent, so I changed to law." Lundgren leaned into the unfinished painting. "He tells a story with brush strokes. What a genius." She looked at Kit. "I know he's a recluse, but I'd be honored to meet him."

It reminded Kit of when Robin told her how critics and docents praised her work at exhibits. But to have someone stand in her studio and express how her art touched them, well, it made her—happy.

"He uses horses a lot," Lundgren said. "My favorite is the Equine Series. You can feel the movement, hear the hooves beating against the ground."

Kit was impressed by the woman's knowledge, her trained eye.

"Where did you meet? In the carnival, or circus? It must have been a hard life."

"Not as bad as home. Carnival came to town, and I ran away. Fourteen years old, a hoochie-coochie girl. It was roughest on the animals and freaks. In 1948, no jobs for women, but I survived." Kit hadn't talked about her life with the carny for years. But like Lundgren said, it showed up in her work, often with horses. "The circus. Then the pin-ups and movies. I survived that too. Not like the other blonde bombshells. So many died— suicides, overdoses. Jayne Mansfield was killed in a car crash." Kit felt fatigued. "Yes," she nodded, "I survived that life, too."

Lundgren listened, but Kit observed her inching her way toward the collage series on the worktable.

"This is an incredible studio. The lighting. High ceilings. Skylights. Everything an artist could dream of. Makes me want to paint again." Lundgren glanced at Muffin lapping water from her bowl and then settle into her bed.

Kit flinched when Lundgren spotted her pink paw-patterned smock draped over the   back of a chair and the unopened pack of Winstons on the worktable.

Lundgren turned slowly. She didn't look at her, just stared off. Kit experienced a shock of her own. She saw Lundgren putting it all together— amazement, then the revelation. Oh shit! What could Kit do about it? Kill her?

Lundgren tidied her short blonde hair behind her ears.

"I need a cigarette." Kit wheeled Sherman toward the door. "C'mon Lundgren. D. L. wouldn't want anyone but me alone with his work," she said, making light of a moment that changed both their lives.

Muffin ran out the door. Kit looked over her shoulder. "You coming?"

Their eyes met. Lundgren's were filled with tears.

"I'm tired. I need to sit down. Coming?"

Kit and Muffin walked down the path to the cactus garden. She figured Lundgren was somewhere behind. Tears. She knew them well. But when others cried, it put her at a disadvantage, made her feel mushy. And the young woman looked so beautiful standing in her studio with the sunlight catching every nuance of understanding that passed over her face.

Kit sat on a wrought iron bench, pulled Sherman close, lighted up, and surveyed her garden.

On a lookout, atop the Palisades, her nearest neighbor somewhere below, she really was a recluse. At eighty-five, with death a kiss away, she'd been angry for decades, for her stepfather's abuse, Daniel's death, even the small slights, building on top of one another making her view of life a vista of loneliness.

Muffin whined. Kit looked up and saw Lundgren. Muffin jumped up on her hind legs begging Lundgren to pick her up. The woman crouched down, petted Muffin, and looked at Kit.

She nodded.

"I have two silkies, I bet she smells them."

"It's more than that." Kit's voice had the tired monotony of a flat tire. It wasn't even noon and she needed a nap. She coughed, hacked, and spit out a glob of phlegm. "Excuse me."

Kit took out her handkerchief and wiped her mouth. "I'm not used to company," she said and continued to smoke.

"Hey, Mom," Robin yelled from the top of the garden path, "Is everything okay?"

"Yes," Lundgren answered for her. "Tell the crew I'll be up in a few minutes." Lundgren handed Muffin to Kit and walked around the garden. Her hair was tousled by the breeze.

Kit preferred her like this—mussed. She wondered what the woman looked like at home, in jeans and a T-shirt. Lundgren walked through the narrow aisles, inspecting the plants.

"They're beautiful how they bloom," she said. "Like a miracle. I love the subtlety of the color, the shape, how the sunlight captures the unexposed side of the petals."

Kit remembered how Lundgren studied the photos on the wall. She was sensitive, with an artist's eye. Maybe she wasn't going to exploit her after all. The pretty blonde with the slender build must have put up with a lot of sexual harassment. If so, Kit doubted she'd share any of it with her. She thought of Lundgren as quiet, low-key, except when she talked about D. L. Hawkins, then she herself bloomed.

"I understand why you had to choose a pseudonym," Lundgren said with her back still to Kit. She turned. "I can't imagine what you went through." Lundgren walked over and sat next to her. "Not just your generation. My mother had me young. My father ran off and the only way she could keep me and get an education was to dance in strip clubs. She made a good living. That was the 1980s. It's still hard."

The two women gazed at the garden with the Pacific as a backdrop.

"There's a way to make everyone forget about your video," Lundgren said.

Kit took a deep inhalation of oxygen, closed her eyes, and savored her last moments as D. L. Hawkins. It was her little champagne-colored poodle who had pulled back the curtain and revealed her identity—Muffin, leading Lundgren down the path to her door, giving her away.

Kit could see it now. Robin would take off her oxygen tube and dance her around the living room, overjoyed that his mom would be coming out of the closet. The thought of his endless euphoria exhausted her, but Lundgren was right. It would wipe that stupid video off the networks and change her name from a verb back to a noun.

She stubbed out her Winston. Leaning on Lundgren, she struggled to her feet.

"I'm going to lie down. Run this by Robin. You guys work out the details. But tell him not to wake me until three. And I'll want my martini extra dry."

Kit shuffled along. She pulled Sherman as the wheels made clap-clap sounds over the yellow brick path, with Lundgren beside her and Muffin running ahead.

LUISA KAY REYES

Biography

Luisa Kay Reyes has had pieces featured in "The Raven Chronicles", "The Windmill", "The Foliate Oak", "The Eastern Iowa Review", and other literary magazines. Her essay, "Thank You", is the winner of the April 2017 memoir contest of "The Dead Mule School Of Southern Literature". And her Christmas poem was a first place winner in the 16th Annual Stark County District Library Poetry Contest. Additionally, her essay "My Border Crossing" received a Pushcart Prize nomination from the Port Yonder Press. And two of her essays have been nominated for the "Best of the Net" anthology. With one of her essays recently being featured on "The Dirty Spoon" radio hour.

Inherited History

"And taking with her nothing but a dress she sewed herself and her own horse, Mariah Ware left her father's white columned plantation to elope with her true love . . ." Lynn smiled as she listened to the nonagenarian Miss Ginger tell the familiar story. For the tale of how her four-greats maternal grandmother had defied her father's wishes to elope with the impoverished Brandon Covington was one Lynn had heard repeated quite often throughout her childhood. For her mother, Kathleen, was the family genealogist and folklorist, so they frequently traveled throughout the barely trodden wilds of the national forest to hunt up some of the elderly ladies who were only too thrilled to welcome someone who was interested in their stories from long ago into their meager wooden dwellings. Being elderly, the small wooden shacks were usually well heated. And today was no exception. For Lynn could feel the beads of perspiration forming along her forehead and falling down the back of her neck, while Miss Ginger appeared to be perfectly content in her flower printed homespun dress reciting the story of Mariah Ware with a small blanket made of yarn resting on her lap.

"Was he very handsome?" Lynn asked, taking everybody by surprise. But it was a question she had often pondered since she was old enough to consider the import of Mariah's elopement. No one ever mentioned whether or not Brandon Covington was possessed of Old Hollywood movie star good looks and Lynn found it hard to believe that Mariah could abandon the more affluent lifestyle her father had to offer for Covington's meager brush arbor without a compelling reason.

"I suppose he was," replied Miss Ginger after a moment's pause. During which time Lynn felt the warning look of "Hush!" boring down on her heavily from her mother's eyes that had become ever more round with astonishment. "But I can't say that I ever heard anybody say so. However, my daddy was the best looking man I ever saw, so it must be so. There's my daddy right there," Miss Ginger said while pointing to a small black and white picture that was hanging on the living room wall, prompting Lynn's mother to jump up and look at it while exclaiming, "Oh, such a dapper looking young man! Don't you think so, Lynn?"

The truth was that Lynn didn't particularly think so. But if she hunted and pecked, there was something appealing by the three piece suit he was wearing and his hat that was placed at an ever so slightly rakish angle, that allowed her to nod somewhat truthfully in agreement. Much to the delight of Miss Ginger who blissfully continued on with the story. "After a while, Dr. Ware relented somewhat and offered Mariah and her husband a cow to help them out. Which they accepted, only because it was for the children."

Now this detail really grabbed the attention of both Lynn and her mother who found themselves sitting up more erectly than before, for this was one tidbit they had not heard before.

"Oh, do tell!" Lynn and her mother both eagerly begged of Miss Ginger. Since it was these unique details that each elderly lady seemed to have that made listening to the old familiar stories of bygone years worth the while.

"But the cow got sick after only one week and passed away," she continued. Leading to sighs of sympathy being expressed all around. "So rather than giving them another cow, Dr. Ware gave them a goat instead, which they kept for several years."

This being another unexpected detail which brought a smile to both Lynn and her mother's faces. And with the warmth of the small living room ever increasing, Lynn reached for her long hair and tossed it behind her shoulders.

"Such pretty hair you have!" Miss Ginger stated with much enthusiasm. Which made Lynn's smile broaden. For the elderly ladies they visited seemed to always comment on her long dark hair. "Which reminds me, I saw y'all's picture on the front page of the newspaper." And reaching underneath some items on her coffee table, Miss Ginger soon retrieved two copies of last Sunday's local newspaper. "Since I knew y'all were comin' I saved mine for you and my neighbor gave me her copy, as well."

"That is so very sweet," Lynn's mother gleefully exclaimed with Lynn concurring. "I was thinking about going to the newspaper office to buy some more copies and now I don't have to. Oh, this is wonderful!" For Kathleen was featured in the foreground and Lynn was featured in the background of the prominent picture on display on the very front of the newspaper. Being part of a property rights group that was questioning the methods the city was using to condemn some houses in an area that was once prominent but had since been upended by bigger and grander homes that were built across the river, Lynn and Kathleen had inadvertently become the faces of the declining hilltop community.

"Well, I certainly think it is a good cause you are fighting for. Those houses look mightily fine to me," Miss Ginger stated, with a heretofore unrevealed inner strength. "And if you need anybody to join you in city hall, count me in!" Causing Lynn to feel some admiration for this plucky old lady. Who then got up to serve them some light refreshments. There was always a little bit of gumption in these elderly ladies that made Lynn wonder if the secret to their long lifespans was this hidden come-what-may determination that they all seemed to possess. At the very least, it didn't appear to do them any harm. Other than to confound their adult sons who were usually only too eager to have them ensconced in a nursing home rather than fool with the tedious chore of feigning filial concern by visiting them briefly once every two weeks or so.

The rest of the afternoon then went by pleasantly. As Lynn and Kathleen partook of Miss Ginger's homemade pecan pie and struggled to keep from fainting out of the ensuing blood sugar drops. But it was always difficult to be anything but light-hearted when talking about family history with these elderly kith and kin. Even if sometimes the family history could tend towards the less than ideal.

"The Wares never forgave Mariah for her elopement and she was eventually disinherited," Miss Ginger continued, back on the original topic.

"We know!" Lynn and Kathleen responded in unison. With Lynn recalling only too vividly the one time they went to an extended Ware family reunion when she was a child. And experienced first-hand the closest thing to an Amish shunning that an "English" person could experience. Even though the Wares weren't Amish, they had mastered the art of snubbing so well, it made one wonder if there wasn't some hidden connection between the two.

"But, my father was still very proud of his Ware ancestry," Miss Ginger commented with the special glow of unreserved admiration on her face that daughters both young and old have when talking about their daddies. "And he even joined the Sons of the American Revolution through his Ware ancestor."

The next evening, Lynn found herself getting ready for the summer young professionals' social. It was a group the city had recently started in order to attract and keep young professionals in the area. With most of Lynn's college friends having moved away several years prior, Lynn decided to attend the event in order to meet some new peers. She was approaching the outermost rim of the age bracket for the young professionals organization, so she decided to cough up the required entry fee for the event and head over to the exclusive rooftop restaurant where the social was being held.

"Have you ever been here before?" the young man taking the entry fees asked Lynn when she approached the sign in table. To which Lynn nodded in the negative, since this was her first time to attend any of the young professionals events. Surprised by her response, he handed her some extra drink tickets with the comment to "make the most of it."

Feeling a little bit unsure as to what to do, Lynn began moseying around the rooftop and looking around. The view of the city's river from the rooftop was certainly impacting. Yet, it seemed like at first, the social was going to be a sparsely attended one. Nonetheless, as time went on, more and more people began filing in. Filling Lynn with wonder, for it had never dawned on her that there were so many young professionals in town. Being an only child, she was always surrounded by her mother and the elderly ladies they visited. So, this was quite a novelty for her. And spotting an empty seat at a table, Lynn walked over there and asked the rest of the people seated there if she could join them. To which they readily agreed.

They seemed congenial enough, but after the basic introductions were made, they soon began talking about college football. *College football . . . in the middle of the summer?* Lynn thought to herself incredulously. The first games weren't even going to begin until the first of September and those were just going to be the throw away games. The one in which the opposing teams would only score one touchdown compared to the seventy points of the athletic powerhouses. And that would only be because the head coaches finally relented and put in their third and fourth string players to give their mainstays a much needed reprieve.

Lynn tried to maintain an interest in the conversation but being more artistically inclined she couldn't summon up anything at all to contribute. So, after a short while, she excused herself and got up to mosey around some more. *I've never really been around young professionals before,* she realized. Making feelings of insecurity set in. She claimed this as her hometown, but as she glanced around the room at the well-dressed crowd that seemed in a state of arrested development from their college fraternity days, Lynn realized that she knew absolutely no one. And upon that realization, she decided to make her way to the restroom and then leave.

Fate intervened, however, since just as she was about to reach the door to the ladies restroom, this jovial looking young man with thick rimmed glasses approached her. He was blending the casual and the professional look by sporting a navy blue suit jacket with some long beige pants.

"Leaving so soon?" he inquired of Lynn. To which Lynn responded in the affirmative.

"At least let me introduce myself first," he replied. Before proceeding to inform her that he was originally from Boston and a professor of law at the university with a special interest in the philosophy of law, an esoteric sounding field. And just when Lynn was about to break into the conversation, one of the hostesses of the event came up and approached him about something or another. Leaving Lynn to find herself standing alone for not the first time that evening.

Should I go on home or try to make another go of it? Lynn asked herself after exiting the ladies' room. And after taking into consideration the pricey entry fee that she had already paid, Lynn concluded that it wouldn't hurt to take one more glance of the river from the rooftop before heading home for good. And while walking around the edge of the rooftop, Lynn found the young law professor from earlier coming up to her excitedly with the statement "You won the drawing! Where were you? They called your name out twice and everything."

"I was in the restroom," Lynn responded.

"Hurry and let them know before they draw someone else's name," he urged her.

So, Lynn hurried over to the sign in table and told them rather abashedly where she had been.

"Glad you are here," they replied. "Just wait a while and Tiffany will get you the gift certificate for two for the restaurant."

Lynn was actually hoping to be able to head home without delay, but the prize sounded like it was worth waiting for. So, she found herself walking around somewhat aimlessly, once again.

"Hey, Jessica! Why don't you two come join us?" this group of three guys, who appeared to be approaching their mid-thirties, sitting at a table asked as Lynn walked past. "It is just us guys and that's boring!"

Lynn didn't know the tallish and thin girl standing close to her whose name she deduced was Jessica, but since she motioned for them to both sit at the table, Lynn joined them. Only to find much to her chagrin that they readily began discussing college football by revisiting with relish last year's championship game as though it were just yesterday.

Jessica adeptly joined right in with the conversation. And for at least fifteen minutes, it felt like Lynn sat there quietly turning her head from left to right like watching the final tennis matches at the Davis Cup as one moment the guy sitting next to her spoke and then the next moment Jessica spoke. Finally, after they had exhausted all there was to say about last year's college football championship, there was an awkward lull in the conversation. Until the guy sitting across from the one next to Lynn, ordered him to go get more drinks for everybody. He hesitated, for he didn't have any more drink tickets. And Lynn happily pulled out her extra tickets for him to use. Most grateful, the guy and then got up to go get some drinks and a bottle of spring water for Lynn.

"The sun is shining in my eyes," the apparent leader of the pack then announced. "So, I'm going to move."

And before Lynn knew it, all of a sudden, he was sitting next to her.

With the third guy who had been rather quiet up until then telling him "Smart move."

I really do have nothing in common with my peers, Lynn realized as she struggled for something - anything - to say to this guy who was now sitting beside her. And after scouring her mind for something to say, she noted that he had on a polo shirt emblazoned with the logo of a local architecture firm. Prompting Lynn to ask him if they worked for that firm. To which he cheerfully replied that he did, while the third guy was interviewing with them tomorrow. Then, just when Lynn was about to try to engage in further conversation, some news about college football popped up on the large television screen that was on the wall of the rooftop restaurant, and the leader of the pack abruptly stood up.

"I'm sorry," he told Lynn. "But when news about college football comes on, I have to discuss it with my buddy." And off he went to hunt up some guy to talk to. Leaving Lynn to notice that he was actually rather tall and muscularly built, albeit bordering on the hefty. With a face that could be considered handsome were it not for his somewhat almond shaped eyes.

But, she was rather taken aback as to what to do next as she and tomorrow's interviewee stared at each other wordlessly. *I sure do hope Tiffany comes soon*, she thought to herself. For once she had the door prize she'd won in hand, she was going to head home, never to return.

Soon, however, the leader of the pack returned and resumed his spot next to her. While the guy who had gone to fetch everyone's drinks returned to find his seat occupied. Grasping at straws for something to talk about, with offseason college football definitely not being her forte, Lynn freely announced that she had been on the front page of the local newspaper. Causing the leader of the pack sitting beside her to immediately begin trembling nervously all over with his hands specifically shaking most tremulously.

"What about?" he asked with a sound of terror in his voice. "Can I see the article? Can you pull it up on your phone?"

Which Lynn swiftly did, in spite of feeling puzzled at his sudden onset of anxiety.

And as soon as she showed him the article, the guy got up and left without uttering a single word, abandoning Lynn. Who was left feeling even further puzzled, but feeling ever so grateful when the guy interviewing with the architecture firm the next day pierced through the troublesome moment with, "Don't mind Zack, he's like that. So, tell me, do you ever listen to any podcasts? I was just listening to one today about how to excel on standardized tests."

It wasn't the most entertaining topic to discuss, but it wasn't last year's college football championship and somehow it enabled Lynn and the interviewee to converse back and forth with ease. And after a few moments of actual engaging conversation that Lynn experienced for the first time with a thrill that evening, Zack returned with the statement that it was time for them to leave. He was sweating profusely with his head covered with a dampness that seemed to have come upon him rather quickly, given that earlier he had been perfectly fine.

Even so, the guy Lynn had just been speaking to rationalized his friend's behavior by repeating his earlier comment of, "Zack is like that." And before they fully departed, Zackary pointedly glanced back at Lynn and with a voice of haughty command stated, "Enjoy your infamy!" Rendering Lynn breathless and speechless.

Never was anyone more relieved than she was when at long last Tiffany approached Lynn with the gift certificate and some other knick knacks that were included in the door prize. Beauty bobbles which Lynn shared with Jessica prior to leaving as speedily as she could.

I definitely don't know how to get along with my peers, she thought to herself. *But now I'm not even sure I **want** to get along with them,* she further surmised. As the mind boggling events of the evening replayed themselves inside of her mind on her way home.

Later that night, when Lynn was struggling to sleep with the weight of the disappointing afternoon haunting her, Lynn's phone dinged with the sound that indicated she had a message on social media. "Phooey!" she declared. "I thought I had figured out how to turn that notification off." And she reluctantly looked to see what the message was. It wasn't from anybody she knew, at least not by name. But then she recognized the picture, it was the law professor. He was inviting her to meet up with him at the local coffee shop tomorrow where it would be easier to sit and talk, if she was willing. He didn't seem like a bad guy. But Lynn's confidence was so shaken by the day's unexpected turn of events, that she set her phone back on her nightstand without sending a reply.

After a while, though, curiosity got the better of her. Since the law professor had looked her up, she'd look up this architecture firm that Zack and the other two were a part of or wanting to be a part of. And as soon as she did, their portfolio revealed that the majority of their projects were with the city.

"Sigh!" Lynn heaved out with tears threatening to stream down her face while a bit of anger broiled in the pit of her stomach simultaneously. That at least explained Zackary's sudden onset of hysteria upon seeing the newspaper article . . . but it still didn't excuse his astounding rudeness.

Lynn perused the website some more and then she came upon it - the announcement naming Zackary Ware as principal architect of the firm.

He's a Ware? Lynn thought to herself, *Unbelievable!* Family history seemed to be repeating itself in a peculiar sort of way. Now Lynn sat straight up in her bed with a proud sense of self rising within her. Maybe the evening's events weren't entirely due to her sense of inadequacy amongst her age bracket. Maybe she could be capable of handling an outing with a peer.

"Yes," she replied to the law professor. "I'd love to meet up with you for coffee!"

Making the disillusionments from earlier in the evening evaporate as they were replaced with the anticipation of the coming day's meetup - one that didn't include meeting up with a Ware.

The End.

GERARD SARNAT

Biography

Gerard Sarnat won the Poetry in the Arts First Place Award plus the Dorfman Prize and has been nominated for a handful of recent Pushcarts plus Best of the Net Awards. Gerry is widely published in academic-related journals plus national and international publications. He's authored the collections Homeless Chronicles (2010), Disputes (2012), 17s (2014), Melting the Ice King (2016).

Gerry is a physician who's built and staffed clinics for the marginalized as well as a Stanford professor and healthcare CEO. Currently he is devoting energy/ resources to deal with global warming. Gerry's been married since 1969 with three kids plus six grandsons, and is looking forward to future granddaughters.

Gerard Sarnat

Mid-Septuagenarian Explorations

Not more about meditation, drugs, sex or family

but rather now perhaps the opposite

as testosterone winds down

and just possibly I find

myself gradually

beginning to

involute.

MELISSA L. ST.PIERRE

Biography

Melissa St.Pierre writes creative non-fiction and has appeared in The Blue Nib, Panoply, and 45 Magazine Women's Literary Journal. She has also performed her work in Listen To Your Mother, a spoken word storytelling showcase. Melissa St. Pierre teaches writing and rhetoric at Oakland University in Rochester Hills, Michigan.

The Older Man

After the first date, I stood in front of the bathroom mirror at work, and I wondered when the other shoe would drop? I had a feeling all along that the relationship I was in would end and end badly. Call it a gut reaction, sixth sense, or just a keen acknowledgement of destiny. It wasn't just the fact that dating someone thirteen years older than me was weird on its own. No, it was the fact that the man I had been dating for nearly a month was waging a war and I was on course to be another casualty.

I'd been hoping to date this particular mistake for two years. We had known each other for years, had mutual friends, and had even attended the same school (although years apart). I'd broken up with my college boyfriend in 2006, and from the moment we split, I had my eyes, and heart, set on the older man.

The college boyfriend was okay, but our relationship had gone awry in ways that I had no desire to fix. Some of his behavior had started to irritate and, in some ways, scare me. I had many voicemails that said variations of, "I know you're on campus. I can see your car. Where are you?"

My Suburban-Detroit university has an infamous parking problem, and the fact that he found my car was something of a feat in and of itself. I left the promise ring he'd given me on the edge of a sink in one of the most popular buildings on campus and walked away from it forever. I hope that it became another woman's and that she desperately loves it.

The older man treated me like a kid-sister for three years, and then by some "miracle," he asked me on a date. We planned to go to favorite restaurant of both of ours.

I agonized over what I was going to wear, down to the shoes. What was I going to say?

What was I going to talk about? The most exciting thing in my life was graduate school. Would he understand? I loved art. Would he know what in the sam hell I was talking about? He liked country music, and I am, at heart, a classic rock chic.

We sat at the bar, and I don't have the slightest idea what we talked about. Then he said, "Is this a date, or are we two friends out for dinner?"

What the crap? I thought this was determined. I have date hair, not "friend" hair. I have date shoes. I WORE MAKEUP!

"Well, what do you want it to be?" God, I was cool. I can't believe that was my response.

I was smart. I was cool. I was 23....

I couldn't believe that this "perfect" older man and I were officially dating, as per our eventual determination. I left that evening believing that a good thing had just begun.

However, intuition and I have always had a remarkable relationship. She and I have kept each other out of many stupid, dangerous, and uncomfortable situations for over thirty years.

Intuition and I are like peas and carrots.

That night, I chose to ignore her.

Ignored point of intuition number one: I was desperately nervous. I paced the floor at home and changed my outfit multiple times. This is strange behavior for me. Although I am a selective extrovert, I am normally fairly confident in my wardrobe selection. I figured that if I was going to feel awkward, I had damn well better kill it with my ensemble. For me, being nervous to change that many times to feel okay was a problem.

Ignored point of intuition number two: On the way to the restaurant, he changed Journey's "Don't Stop Believing" to another song, one that I didn't know and didn't like. This even after I jumped in the seat saying "oh! I love this song!" in response to Steve Perry's stunning vocal styling.

Ignored point of intuition number three: It came as a surprise to our mutual friends that we were dating. They thought he was still seeing his "former" (as told to me) girlfriend, Amy.

They knew nothing of our relationship.

It all came crashing down just over a month into the relationship. We sat in his living room, watching an episode of a pointless reality show. He had been quiet all evening, which I didn't think too odd at the time. But when he finally looked at me and spoke, he used a mouse like, un-manly voice, and nearly whispered, "You're a virgin aren't you?"

My feet went cold. Where the actual hell had that come from? I didn't know why, but I was instantly defensive. But I looked at him and replied confidently, "Yes. Why, is that a problem for you?" He muttered a reply that I can't remember but it made the mood sour.

"I'm going home." I stood up and announced about twenty minutes later. And without any protest from the older man, I left. We didn't make plans to see each other.

I spent the thirty-minute drive home thinking about his question. Where had that come from? I was pissed. Why was this even a question?

It hit me, kind of stupidly, in the forehead. I was hidden from his life. Our friend didn't know. We only went out on Mondays, when the chances of seeing people we both knew were significantly reduced. He didn't ask me much. Listened to me talk, I think... but didn't get me. I was, again, to be a "conquest."

Screw. That.

Did he really think that after three years of treating me like a younger sister, and four weeks officially "dating," that it was time to take that step? Did I even want to? It seemed so in from left field. He hadn't pressured me, and it wasn't a "heat of the moment" question. I was watching some show that I detested and remember counting the ways I found it's "contestants" pathetic and drippy.

I was a twenty-first century woman with my own ideas about my body, my emotions, my choices, commitment, and what defined me. If he thought this was going to be a casual decision that I was going to make on the spot, he was wrong. That I knew. Regardless of how much, and how long, I had adored him. I had adored myself longer and I loved my self-worth more than I could have ever loved him.

And there was the key word, and I asked myself again, did I even want to take that step with the older man?

The answer was no.

Several days passed and we didn't talk to each other. I was still under the illusion that we were in this "relationship" and it would be fine. I was prepared to "explain" (read: defend) because that's what it would have looked like my decisions. But, yeah, that relationship would be just friggin' dandy.

I looked in the bathroom mirror at work and knew. This is when the shoe would drop.

And I was right.

I climbed the stairs back to my desk and found a text on my phone. A text. On my phone.

And it read, "I think we need to take a break." I spun in my chair, unsure what to do or how to take this revelation. What did that mean? Ross and Rachel took a break and look what happened to them!

"What the hell does that even mean?" I text back. I never received an answer.

He never gave me an answer, but I knew he had unceremoniously "dumped" me because

I had no intention of entering into a casual sexual relationship with him.

That evening was the last time we had a private conversation.

I later learned after that evening the older man embarked in the kind of foolish behavior that one is accustomed to seeing in spoiled children.

I received a myriad of name calling and mud-slinging. To the mutual friends we had, I became "crazy." I was nuts for always sending him birthday cards. I was "insane." I was a "stalker." I was a "slut." To him, I was everything that I wasn't in reality. His reality was one in which women's characters could be colored to his liking. He wanted mine the color of burned charcoal.

I wondered why our mutual friends wouldn't look me in the eye and walked away when I came near them. What is truly sickening? I didn't find any of this out on my own. I heard it through the metaphorical grapevine only later to have it confirmed. Everything I heard Connor had done, he did.

Ninety-nine percent of our mutual friends believed him. They had known me since I was ten years old, and they believed this man that degraded me.

I didn't find out until years after the fact that only one, managed to stand up to the older man and tell him, "You're full of shit."

This is how easy it is to believe falsehoods about women: if one man says it…it must be true. My truth, women's truth, be damned.

In late 2011, I saw the older man. By then, I was 26 years old. He was pushing 40. Hard.

I was happily cruising through a local grocery store buying provisions for a meal I was hosting at my home.

As I turned and headed into the pasta aisle, I heard the unmistakable scream of a gecko. I looked up from my list, and there was the older man. Staring at me and smiling like we'd seen each other the day before and were old friends.

"Hey, Melissa, how are you?"

I didn't hate this man, but I damn sure didn't like him. He'd had the nerve to send me a Facebook friend request. Really.

There are reasons why I am friends with exactly one person I dated. The older man wasn't good enough to be a speck of dirt on that one person's shoe. Never was. Never will be.

"I'm great, thanks." I could feel bile in my mouth and had to fight the urge to throw up on his shoes.

We made small talk for about thirteen seconds before the vomit threshold began to wane.

"Yea, well, I'll see ya later, nice to see you, Melissa."

See me later? He had a better chance of an alien probe. And for the second time, I turned my back to him and left him alone in the pasta aisle without another word.

He had the nerve to look "wounded."

He deserved nothing from me. I didn't give him the information that he so desperately wanted. Insight into my life—my "progression" from him.

There are many things that I could have said to him. Many of those words could have been powerful words and some could have an "f" and the "u" standing prominently at the front.

By the time I finally saw him face to face, it wasn't worth the trouble. I didn't need to bring up the actions of a sophomoric piece of rock that wasn't worth a millisecond of a prisoner's time, much less mine.

When I saw him, I was given the opportunity to speak my truth without words. I didn't have to tell him that he was a liar. He knew.

And although being silent is hardly what I would tell another woman in my shoes, my silence that day in the pasta aisle, spoke more to him than words would have. Because for the second time, I wouldn't change who I was to fit his wants. I didn't give him what he thought he deserved. And if to him, I am a frigid bitch, that's fine.

I will live to be called worse by a whole lot better.

JAMES SANCHEZ

Biography

James Sanchez is a poet and a teacher from Hialeah, Florida. He holds a B.A. in English from Florida International University. He teaches English and Creative Writing at Ronald W. Reagan Senior High School in Doral, Florida. He resides in Miami, Florida with his wife and son. His work has been published in The Acentos Review, The Apeiron Review, The Circle Review, Blue Heron Review and Lost Coast Review, Muddy River Poetry Review, and The Northampton Poetry Review.

James Sanchez

Ash

I do not think of him in hospice care,
staring oblivion in the eye, prepping for nothing; hoping for
one last call.

The wind through the trees; the water through the years.

The fire dead before dawn.
The river trout long since digested.
Her clothes scattered near the tent.
What now?
Another sip from the flesh, one more drag from the
cigar. The mountains rise, jaguar teeth.
My teeth crimson and fine.
Months of grinding
She doesn't know—can't know, but she must know.
My touch quicker
My looks subtler
My memory fleeting
I loved her once
When these mountains were new, but now they are
as old as they have ever been.
There once was a fire, but that was well before
dawn.

James Sanchez

Fingerprint

I still hold out hope that your scent will linger.
The aroma of your skin will poke and prod at me like reasons.
It is not obsession; I promise you.
It is hope wrapped in the fine paper of last chances.
You walked me cross the Quad years ago in the snow. Insane,
I know, but I can still make out the snowflakes-- Not intricate,
but an amorphous collection of tears.
I walk alone these days more than ever before
I sense the people around me

I long for you.

She sips her coffee in between breaths.
Last night, the anniversary, the candles lay
against a chipped dish. His kiss lingers
As if memory had a conscience.
Texas in the fall smells of smoke and musk.
She won't follow him.
She sips her life in between doubts.
Today, the beginning, the car keys splayed next to a tattered
purse.
Her touch persists like a fingerprint in grease.

James Sanchez

Prayer

I have no more lines for you.
My offerings dull, sour lacking imagination.
Inarticulate prayers,
Misheard,
Misunderstood, Misplaced.
Dim-witted scribe Writing verses for no one.
No words,
No rhymes, No syllables Worthy of hearing.
Failure then. Failure now.
Failure forever.
Scribbling nonsense onto unwitting pages No purpose Only
mechanics and habit.

Would it be more convenient for you, If I lived in dreams alongside
purple dragons?
On fields of clay?
Speak to me!
Words like sickles, Tear at the root of all-- Misery.
In the jungle
The snakes coil around rubber trees,
While the lumberjacks hack away beauty.
You too, my dear disregard truth and question sincerity.
Under the stars
Tonight, I will sleep with your memory. Toss and turn with your
scent, Flail about with your vision.
Only in dreams
Do we breathe the righteous air.

To you I seem old in my coat and tie,
Sipping cooling coffee,
Bought with recent change; once, I was young, younger than that
smirk, Younger than that contempt.
I rode horses in a circus decade before your first sneer.
I met her along the river. We made love by a rented moon.
Dreamed of children running through reimagined homes, but to
you I seem old. What do I know about love?
The cost of a kiss?
The cost of a glance across a classroom?

DON NOEL

Biography

Retired after four decades' prizewinning print and broadcast journalism in Hartford CT, I received my MFA in Creative Writing from Fairfield University in 2013. I have since published more than five dozen short stories and non-fiction pieces but have two novellas and a novel still looking for publishers.

Bonding

Gerry was steamed when his son arrived at the funeral home wearing that baseball cap. Not that it was unusual: He'd been a royal pain in the ass recently. Teen-age rebellion, Laura said. Hard to believe this was the boy who'd loved practicing baseball with his Papa.

Dozens were in line to pay last respects; more were in the foyer signing the sympathy book. His Gretchen lay there, on her right hand the Claddagh ring they'd bought in Ireland last year just before she fell ill. Love, loyalty, friendship. His heart ached.

The room was banked with flowers – from the teachers' union, school staff, PTA, food bank, homeless shelter, Boy and Girl Scouts, bridge club. Half of Middletown.

People wore their Sunday best. Gerry was stuffed into a suit he hadn't worn in years. If Gretchen were alive, she'd have let it out; she was a terrific seamstress. In fact, Laura wore a dark dress that Gretchen re-tailored for her to start college two years ago. She looked so much like her mother. The rest in the receiving line, his brother Marvin and Gretchen's siblings and their spouses, were dressed formally.

And here came Jeremy, skulking in and squeezing next to his sister, in cut-off jeans and a long-sleeved red jersey, his hair spilling out of a baseball cap on which was lettered Life has no meaning. At least it was turned sideways; people might not notice the words.

"We're going to miss her," Mrs. Murphy was saying. "If there's anything we can do . . ."

"Thank you," he said, trying not to sound hurried. "Laura, this is Mrs. Murphy from the food pantry." He stepped behind her to face Jeremy. "For God's sake, take that off!"

Mistake. When Jeremy turned his head, the bill pointed forward, the gold-on-black lettering standing out like neon. "People have come to pay respects to your mother," Gerry hissed. "Why can't you be respectful?"

"I didn't even want to be here. It's bullshit. None of this will bring Mama back."

Gerry could almost hear Gretchen: *Lay off, dear. He's quick to anger; he learned that from you.* He turned to Marvin, next in line, Jeremy's favorite uncle. "Can you try? I've got to greet people."

"Hey," Marvin said, laid-back, calm, a hand on Jeremy's shoulder, "glad you're here."

His son turned, and more of the quote showed: no meaning. . . the moment you lose . . . something. So many words on a cap! Just above the bill was a name: Jean-Paul somebody. Have to ask Laura what that's about.

Gerry hurried back in line to accept condolences from Mrs. Wadsworth. "So young. A tragedy. A few months ago, at the women's shelter, she looked so well. It was cancer?"

"Pancreatic."

"I'm so sorry. I suppose at the end that was a blessing."

"Thank you." He handed her on to Laura, remembering those hard final weeks, the hospice staff helping them accept the inevitable.

All but Jeremy, who came only once. He'd begun playing video games in his room: *Carmageddon, Mortal Kombat, Thrill Kill.* When Gerry made him turn the volume down at night, he skipped school to play during the day. Gerry, going to the hospice early and then to work, didn't know until the school called.

"Jeremy," he said that night, "Your Mama wants to know if you're keeping up your studies." Untrue: He hadn't wanted to burden Gretchen.

"Lie to her," Jeremy had said. Defiant. Didn't even pretend, let alone promise to do better.

Mrs. Howarth stepped up now and gave him a hug. His neighbor's mother, a retired guidance counselor. "It's going to be hard." She looked meaningfully down the line at Jeremy.

"Thank you."

The wake went another hour. Marvin had persuaded Jeremy to take off the hat and to say just "Thank you," to mourners. After a while, that became "Thank you, it doesn't matter," which made Gerry mad all over again, but most didn't seem to hear it. *The ritual of funerals doesn't demand full attention*, he thought.

At last, the line finished. Jeremy disappeared, wearing the cap. The undertaker took the casket to some cold dark soulless refrigerator until the funeral the next day; Gerry didn't want to think about that. A dozen were still seated in the room, praying. He should thank them. Sitting down with each would encourage lingering, but God surely didn't mean a man his size to stand in a tight suit for two hours straight.

First, Mrs. Howarth. "Jeremy is troubled," she said.

"We used to be close," he told her. "He's probably home playing video games."

"It's hard to cope with a mother's death. We'll have you over for dinner."

"Just a matter of time," Marvin butted in. "He'll get past it. Kids are resilient."

"Call me," she said to Gerry.

Agnes Hardy had tarried. And Muriel Butler. Both widowed early. A good mechanic in a small town knows people by their cars. Jack left Agnes a 1999 Riviera. Charlie left Muriel a newer BMW. Both kept coming to him. "I'm so sorry about Gretchen," Agnes said at the garage one day. "Cancer is cruel. Tell me if I can do anything to help." She paused for emphasis: "Anything at all."

Now she patted a chair when he reached her side of the room. "It will be a difficult time. Lonely. Call when you'd like a home-cooked meal."

"Thank you," he said, getting up.

Muriel smiled from across the room. She'd been even less subtle. Called one evening: Her car, which she needed first thing in the morning, wouldn't start. He stopped on his way from the hospice. It started right away. "It must be hard," she said, unapologetic, "working all day, spending time with her, coming home tired and alone." He said he'd send a bill and left.

"Dear Gerry, you must be distraught," she said now.

"Thank you."

"And lonely. You'll call me when the time seems right." She said it more like a forecast than an invitation.

He looked around, wondering if Laura had noticed these two, glad Jeremy had left. He finished his goodbyes and went to Mario's Ristorante, where Marvin had reserved a room. "To be family together," he said. "Celebrate her life and remind ourselves that life must go on."

Jeremy didn't come.

"Did you see his hat?" Gerry asked Laura.

"I know. Embarrassing. Poor Jeremy."

"What was it all about?"

"It's by Jean-Paul Sartre. I'm afraid he got it from me."

"Who?"

"A French philosopher, Papa. I studied him and brought the book home. Jeremy borrowed it. I'd probably bookmarked that quote. It's famous."

"I didn't know you could get so many words on a hat."

"There's a shop downtown. They do customized."

"What does the whole thing say?"

"Let's see. 'Life has no meaning the moment you lose the illusion of being eternal.' Something like that."

"Too complicated for me. Doesn't sound optimistic."

"It isn't, Papa. Did Mrs. Naismith talk to you?"

"No."

"She didn't tell you about the cat?"

"Her tomcat that yowls all night? I haven't heard it recently."

"She thinks Jeremy killed it. She found it on her doorstep one morning, sort of . . . mutilated. He needs help, Papa. We should get him to a psychiatrist."

"He doesn't need a shrink," said Marvin, butting in again.

"I think he does, Uncle Marvin."

"Give him time."

When he and Laura got back to the house, the noise from upstairs was deafening. "I'll go talk with him, Papa."

He listened from the living room. They'd been close; maybe she could get through to him. The racket stopped. Low voices. The video started again, but quieter. Laura stopped in the kitchen, came back with cheese and crackers and red wine just like Gretchen used to do.

"Have you seen the cuts on his arms, Papa?"

On his arms? Jeremy had worn only long-sleeved shirts recently. "Cuts? No."

"Razor cuts, I think."

"He's shaving his arms? Why would he do that?"

"Not shaving. He's cutting himself. We read about it in Psych 101. People feel numb and cut themselves to feel pain."

"I guess you were right about getting a psychiatrist."

"It won't be easy."

"Maybe Mrs. Howarth next door can help. I'll talk to her."

They fell silent. Gerry considered going upstairs. If Jeremy came to the door, he might see the razor cuts.

"Papa," Laura said, "you should get rid of the guns." His two rifles and the shotgun were in a mahogany wall cabinet that Gretchen found. "You don't use them anymore."

"No. I pay my dues but haven't even been to target practice." He looked at the cabinet, so cleverly made that an intruder might think it held teacups. "It's locked. So is the night table where I keep the pistol."

"Papa, anyone could bust in with a screwdriver."

"I'll think about it."

He did think about it. Couldn't get to sleep. Tried to imagine cutting his arms with a razor blade. Couldn't even imagine how addicts stuck needles into themselves.

The funeral service next day was awful. The parson went through the pious stuff about Gretchen's being in a better place now. People came to the pulpit to praise her. Laura made him teary saying what a good mother she was, telling about the time the cocker spaniel ate all the Easter eggs, which made him laugh through the tears. He wished Jeremy had come. A little reluctant laughter might do him good. Like the time he broke his leg sliding into second base and learned to smile through the pain.

He wished Gretchen could hear it all. By the time everyone finished, Gerry was blowing his nose so hard that no one expected him to go up there too.

Most of them came to the burial. It was a blue-skied fall morning, leaves just turning. The parson read more scripture, the casket was lowered, and he and Laura threw the first handfuls of dirt with a mournful thunk! After others threw some dirt, the parson ended the ceremony and led them away so they wouldn't see the cemetery workmen fill the grave.

Walking back through the depressing hundreds of gravestones, Gerry glimpsed someone standing with head bent at some other grave. Then he recognized the cap. He let the others go ahead and called. "Jeremy?" He stepped in that direction.

"Let me do it my way, Papa." Jeremy's voice had a hollow ring. "You don't know what it's like."

Some inner demon, Gerry thought. But he'd managed to communicate. "You coming to lunch at Mario's this time?"

"Maybe, Papa."

At least he was saying Papa. Maybe Marvin was right: Give him time. "Everyone would like to see you."

Jeremy shrugged, took off the cap and bowed like some medieval peasant, then walked toward Gretchen's grave. Gerry wanted to follow, but the others were waiting.

Jeremy didn't come to the restaurant. The meal went on too long. Afterward, all the relatives gave hugs and started back to wherever they'd come from. He and Laura came back to the house. No sign of Jeremy.

"He's depressed," Laura said. "See if those guns are still in the cabinet, Papa."

The key was on the mantel under a porcelain shepherd Gretchen bought somewhere. The guns were still there, but she wasn't satisfied. "Why don't you deal with them now? I'll begin putting Mama's clothes in boxes for the women's shelter. You've dreaded that job."

So, she, bless her heart, went up to the bedroom while he took the guns out and unscrewed the cabinet. It seemed weird, having just buried his wife, but kept his mind occupied. He put everything in the trunk and took it to Herb's Sport Shop.

Herb, once a hunting buddy, with a 2009 Accord, offered condolences and said he could probably sell the cabinet and rifles together; he'd take care of the paperwork. "Jeremy was in the other day," he added. "They grow up so fast."

"Jeremy? Did he buy anything?"

"No. Didn't stay long. Wearing a baseball cap with weird lettering. If he wants a gun, why aren't you just giving him yours?"

"I'm not sure he should have a gun." Gerry hesitated. "He's . . . a little unstable sometimes. You saw that hat."

"I could only read part of it. You think he. . ." -- this time it was Herb who hesitated – "might do himself harm?"

"His sister thinks so. I don't want to leave these in his path."

"Gotcha. If he buys from me, he'll have to pass a background check, anyway."

"But seventeen-year-olds can buy guns?"

"Anyone can have a long gun, Gerry. Twenty-one to get a handgun or a carry permit."

"If he comes back, have a talk. Like, ask where he's hunting."

"Sure, Gerry."

"Not like quizzing, you know? Just conversation."

"I understand."

"And give me a call, will you?"

By the time he got back, Laura had found something to cover the faded wallpaper behind the gun cabinet: a huge painting Gretchen bought at an auction when they vacationed in Vermont years ago, an autumn maple with white birches and dark pines. Once home, she'd decided it was too big, and consigned it to the attic.

"It's as though she knew we'd need that huge painting someday, Papa. It's perfect."

It wasn't really. It overpowered the living room. But it reminded him of Gretchen.

Laura had most of the clothes in cardboard boxes and had some earrings and brooches and necklaces on the coffee table. "Papa, I'd like to keep these. To wear in remembrance, you know? And to pass on as family heirlooms."

"Sure," he said. "Your Mama would want that." He was still worrying about Jeremy. "Anything your brother might want?"

"How about this locket?" Laura opened a little heart on a gold chain. "It's you and Mama and a baby. Must be one of us."

"Perfect. It's Jeremy. Someone took the photo at the hospital. I bought the locket and gave it to her the day she brought him home."

They didn't tell Jeremy about the locket right away. He got home just after they got the boxes piled by the door for the shelter people and were in the living room with cheese and crackers and wine.

"Come join us, bro," Laura said.

"You took down the gun cabinet."

"Papa's starting a new life. He wasn't using them."

"I was."

"What do you mean, you were?" Gerry said.

"Just target practice. Out in the woods."

So much for locked cabinets and hidden keys, Gerry thought. "You didn't ask."

"Didn't think I needed to."

Gerry wanted to ask why the hell he would think that but held his temper. He was frightened as well as angry.

Jeremy changed the subject. "Where did you get that picture? It looks like the cemetery."

"Mama bought it in Vermont," Laura said. "It's been in the attic."

"It's ugly."

"It's a remembrance. You and Papa will have to cheer each other up."

"Sure. See you in the morning."

"Wait! We went through Mama's stuff and found something you might want."

"I saw the boxes by the door."

"That just clothes. I mean here on the coffee table."

"Looks like jewelry. What are you going to do, sell it?"

"No, silly. Mama never had really expensive jewelry. These are keepsakes, to pass along to our children."

"If you have kids."

"I will, someday. Won't you?"

"Hell, no!"

Gerry cleared his throat to speak, but Laura flapped her hand to silence him exactly the way Gretchen used to. "Well, we found a locket that might change your mind."

"What do you mean, a locket?"

"Here, look."

"God, Mama looks so young. Who's the baby?"

"It's you. At the hospital just after you were born."

"Ugly even then, wasn't I?"

"No! You're not ugly. Your eyes remind me of Mama."

"I don't want to be reminded about Mama. She's gone. I'm going to bed."

But he took the locket with him as he trudged noisily up the stairs.

Sunday morning, Laura insisted on making bacon and waffles like Gretchen used to. "Oh, Papa," she said as she gave him a second helping, "you'll have to tell Grandpa Harry. Do you want me to stay another day to come with you?"

Just then Jeremy dragged in. He was still in pajamas, which were long-sleeved so Gerry couldn't see his arms, but the top was only half-buttoned, and he had the locket around his neck. "It won't matter," he broke in. "The old man won't get it anyway. He's like totally out of it."

Harry Peters was indeed in a locked wing at the convalescent home, although Gerry thought he was too frail to wander even if he tried. The nurses had to drag along his oxygen, on a rolling rack, when they got him out of bed for a daily walk down the hallway and back.

"Not totally," Laura said. Harry had always been her favorite grandparent. She wanted to be an architect because he'd been a carpenter building houses. "He snaps out of it sometimes to ask me how school is going."

"Never lasts long."

"You're right. I guess when he comes to, he remembers Grandma and lets his mind slip away because he can't stand thinking about her."

"I get that."

"Denial. He's despondent. We read about it my college course. He's lost hope."

"I get that too."

Gerry didn't want to get into that conversation. Depressing. Harry's wife died at about Gretchen's age, and the old man never got over it. His mind went first, and then his lungs and legs. Gerry wondered if he'd deteriorate like that. Maybe taking up with one of those widows would stave it off. God! What was he thinking about, at a time like this?

"Maybe you could go with Papa," Laura was saying to Jeremy. "Help explain. He ought to know."

"Okay," Jeremy said.

That was unexpected. "Thank you!" Gerry said, almost too enthusiastically.

"That would be wonderful, bro," Laura said. "Papa will need some moral support."

"Okay."

"You should go before lunch, when sometimes he's more alert."

"Okay. Let's go today."

Maybe Marvin was right: time, and the resilience of youth. Gerry wished Laura could stay longer. Like Gretchen, she'd always been able to cajole Jeremy into a better mood.

"We can take you to the airport," Jeremy said, "and then go from there to – what's its name?"

"Rose Garden Convalescent," Laura said.

"Yeah. Convalescent. As if anyone there was getting better."

"Some do, I think."

"Promise them a Rose Garden," Jeremy said.

A half-hour later they were on their way to the airport in the family Camry. Jeremy actually volunteered to go upstairs for Laura's roll-on and put it in the trunk. Amazing. Only visited Gretchen once in the hospice but was ready to come see his grandfather. He offered to sit in back, but Laura insisted his longer legs needed the room.

"Sit next to Papa," she said. "He needs you."

"Okay," Jeremy said. Sounded almost cheerful. And when they got to the airport, he jumped out to get Laura's bag.

"You don't need to wait." She gave Jeremy a huge, long hug. "Go see Grandpa. Give him my love."

"If he remembers us."

"He will."

She turned, and Gerry welcomed her embrace, her warmth. So much like Gretchen. He swallowed hard and gave her a kiss on the forehead. "Thank you, baby. Stay in touch."

"I will. I'll phone. You two go along now."

Gerry pulled off the road as soon as they got out of the airport complex. It would be a quiet country road to the convalescent home, not much traffic. Jeremy had a learner's permit. "You want to drive?"

"Thanks." He got out the passenger side and came around so that Gerry could just slide over. He was wearing a long-sleeved shirt. "I don't remember the way. You be the navigator."

"It's not far," Gerry said. "Turn left at the next stop sign." Not far from the convalescent home was a baseball field. In his mind he'd mapped a route to pass it. Jeremy drove cautiously and well and recognized the field when they reached it.

"Didn't we used to play here?"

"We did. Stop a minute." They got out of the car to contemplate the field.

"It's small," Jeremy said. "I didn't remember it was so small."

Gerry thought he saw bloodstains on the shirtsleeves. "You were smaller then too, you know. Little League size."

"The Murphy Ford Yankees. This was their home field." Jeremy led the way across right field to first base. "You were a good coach. We beat them."

"We did. Two or three times."

"Mama sat on the other side of that fence behind first base."

"Yes. A half-dozen mothers sat there. Some of them were at the funeral."

"Mama cheered every time I caught the ball."

"And when you got a hit."

"I remember. I hit a home run here and thought she'd jump over the fence."

Gretchen, the proud mother. Supportive mother. They stood silently, remembering. Gerry was sure now they were bloodstains. He finally found words. "Can I see your cuts?"

"No, Papa, please. I'm not proud of them."

Why do you do that, he wanted to ask. "I can't imagine cutting myself," he said instead. "It must hurt."

"The pain tells me I'm still alive."

Just like Laura said, Gerry thought. "Suppose you could talk about it with Mrs. Howarth next door? She was a guidance counselor."

"Maybe later. Let's go see Grandpa."

They drove the rest of the way in silence. Jeremy parked, and they walked to the front desk to be let into the Memory Wing. Most residents were slumped in wheelchairs that the staff had parked in their doorways so they might talk to one another, but none seemed to be talking.

There were few other visitors. Gretchen used to come back feeling sorry for these people. "Almost no one comes to see them, Gerry," she'd say. "I try to brighten their day by making eye contact and smiling and saying good morning." Gerry tried to smile as he and Jeremy threaded past the wheelchairs to reach Harry's room at the end of the hallway. A few smiled back, but mostly he got back vacant stares.

Harry was parked in his doorway too, half-asleep, slouched in a wheelchair to which his oxygen tank was strapped, tubes over his shoulders and into his nose.

Jeremy suddenly seemed impatient to get this over with. "Hello, Grandpa," he said abruptly. "I'm Jeremy."

Harry jolted awake. "Who?" He had macular degeneration, too.

"Jeremy. With my Papa."

"I knew a Jeremy. Younger than you. Used to come with my daughter."

"Yeah."

Gerry thought he'd better get into it. "Good morning, Harry. It's me, Gerry. Gretchen's husband. Jeremy has grown since you saw him."

The old man looked up, one eye squinting, the other once-bushy eyebrow raised like a thin question mark. The quizzical look dissolved into a scowl. "Where's Gretchen?"

"That's what we came to tell you, Grandpa. Mama is dead." Jeremy sounded angry.

"That's why she didn't come with you?"

It hadn't sunk in. "We buried her yesterday," Gerry said. "In the family plot with your wife Myrtle." This was harder than he'd expected. "We came to tell you."

"Dead?"

"Yes. I'm sorry."

The old man closed his eyes, and his head fell to his chest. His shoulders sagged, then rose and fell. He looked up. "Myrtle and Gretchen are both dead?"

"Yes, Harry." Gerry couldn't think what more to say, then tried some of the parson's words. "They're in a better place."

"If you believe that," Jeremy said.

Gerry wanted to believe it. "The pastor said they're both with God," he said.

"What kind of God is that?" Harry demanded. The surliness in the old man's voice matched Jeremy's. He looked down the hallway. "Take two good women in their prime, and leave me here, a useless vegetable?"

"We love you," Gerry said.

"They're both dead?"

"Yes," Jeremy said.

"And why am I still here?"

"Beats me, Grandpa."

Gerry tried to soften it. "God must have a plan," he managed.

"Some plan," Harry said. He fell silent. "Why didn't Gretchen come with you?"

"She's dead," Gerry said. "That's what we came to tell you."

"Oh, yes." The face was gray, stubbly. They must shave him later in the day. A sodden lump of flesh in which nothing works very well but hair still grows, Gerry thought. Keeps growing even after death, he read somewhere. He pushed that thought aside.

An aide appeared with a trolley cart of cookies and cartons of milk and juice. "Morning snack, Mr. Peters. Milk or OJ?" She deftly released the brakes and pushed his wheelchair into the room and under a bed-table.

"Milk, I guess. Just leave it there."

They should stay and help him – Gretchen would have -- but Gerry couldn't think how to help a man eat a cookie. "We've got to get along now, Harry."

Jeremy was obviously more than ready. "Later, Grandpa."

The rheumy old eyes seemed to focus. "Okay," he said. "Why was it you came?"

Gerry couldn't say it again. "Goodbye, Harry."

Neither could Jeremy. "Goodbye, Grandpa."

All the wheelchairs had been pushed into rooms for snacks, and Jeremy strode down the long hallway ahead of him. Gerry hurried to keep up. There was only one Gretchen, no lonely widow could take her place, and he couldn't stand the thought of being like Harry Peters.

"That was a bitch," Jeremy said when they got outside.

"It was."

"Do you really believe in God, Papa?"

"I'm not sure."

"Not me. No God worth praying to would leave people like that. Inmates. Rotting."

"I know what you mean."

This time Jeremy drove too fast. Gerry wanted to say slow down but bit his tongue. "It's getting late," he said when they reached the edge of town. "How about we stop at a drive-in for burgers to take home?"

"Okay. We've shot the day."

The girl at the pay window recognized Jeremy. "I'm sorry about your mother."

"I guess," he said. "Thanks."

"Girl from school?" Gerry asked as they pulled into traffic. "You weren't very friendly."

"No. I was thinking about Grandpa."

When they got home, Jeremy took his burger and shake to his room to eat while he played a video game at blistering volume. Gerry didn't want to make a scene; they'd made progress. He sat alone at the kitchen table where he and Gretchen usually ate. The burger was dry, and he threw most of the fries into the garbage.

In the night table drawer were some earplugs he'd used long ago on the firing range. He took a sleeping pill, poured himself a bourbon, and finally slept.

He woke early, thinking for a moment he would go to the hospice, then realizing that was over. Easy for Marvin to say 'life must go on,' Marvin still had his wife.

He let Jeremy sleep in. Saturday, so it didn't matter. He stopped for donuts and was at the garage by eight, putting on coveralls. There were three cars in the yard, keys slipped through the mail slot. He put the first in the dock, a Ford Fusion. It was good to have something to do. Give the torque wrench in his hand full attention so he didn't screw up someone's engine. He couldn't imagine life without Gretchen. What was the word Laura used? Despondent.

He was working on the Chevy Blazer by noon and turned on the radio to hear the weather. Instead, there was a bulletin. A rampage at Rose Garden Convalescent home. The shooter killed six people in an Alzheimer's wing, but saved the final bullet for himself. Reporters on the way; details soon.

Gerry sat down heavily. He didn't have the stomach for another funeral. Not one; two. Saying farewell to Harry Peters would be no problem but putting Jeremy into the ground next to Gretchen would be incomprehensible.

He thought about the gun in the night table drawer, and knew it surely wasn't there.

PATRICIA WALSH

Biography

Patricia Walsh was born and raised in the parish of Mourneabbey, Co Cork, Ireland. To date, she has published one novel, titled The Quest for Lost Eire, in 2014, and has published one collection of poetry, titled Continuity Errors, with Lapwing Publications in 2010. She has since been published in a variety of print and online journals. These include: *The Lake; Seventh Quarry Press; Marble Journal; New Binary Press; Stanzas; Crossways; Ygdrasil; Seventh Quarry; The Fractured Nuance; Revival Magazine; Ink Sweat and Tears; Drunk Monkeys; Hesterglock Press; Linnet's Wing, Narrator International, The Galway Review; Poethead and The Evening Echo.*

Patricia Walsh

Exalted Vermin

Stuck at rehearsing, arriving too late,
thematic considerations carve out an audience,
captive applause meaning something at last
the scandal sheets drive from the satisfaction.

Sick of androgyny, carved out separately,
the suicidal aftermath never washes nicely,
the probable streetscapes badly realised,
advertise, then sell, all that is good for.

the incinerated wick awaits the light becoming,
the comfort of the night shows infinite promise,
on guard on the time, coffee-grinding promise,
forgetting the obvious, children knowing better.

massacring local inspiration, picking at skin,
pitching in now and again, eschewing alcohol
under a kind of duress, ogling the waitresses
hardened Catholics through no fault of their own.

Murdered for misdemeanor, stuck on a loop,
purchasing stock in trade, consubstantial with the father,
redeemed through excavation of a timely sort,
forgetting time frames of a higher order.

Awarded to minion's clothing, expressions aside,
catching up to the plate, overburdened, exorbitant,
the interesting veneer of sobriety collides
working hard to no effect, loudly stonewalled.

Patricia Walsh

Passing-Through Phase

This is insulation of the highest order,
not rhyming or stealing, the poor things,
the moderate swell of the ashen collective,
mocked to oblivion, a heavy diet goes forth,
cited, that is it, nearly related to division.

rolling out suicide as a revenge tool,
reading into situations a choice discipline,
good, but could be better, floriate temporarily,
the sticky likelihood must ask for a hard station
solace indoors remembered through misdeeds.

Cruelty free, as if that ever existed,
the knowing glances in doorways corridor again,
dispensing a poison no proper one can match,
nice and waterish diet extends to lunchtimes,
the exclusion zone gets wider by the day.

Hoping for a minor miracle, turnaround spite,
not wanted on the food chain anymore,
stock-in-trade jokes going for a song
covered versions suddenly no longer funny,
abdicating love where least expected.

This murmured explosion garbles its purpose,
exclusive singalongs dying off, by degrees,
to listen to oneself is proof of melancholy,
nailed to a proper cross, real wood, mind!
Victimized leanings reward for a pride.

Patricia Walsh

Excellent Security

The watching brief, crippled by finite tears,
attention sought and given, writing by the book,
the senile associates watched for shame again,
followed footsteps watched in a sneaky fashion.

Fattened exit from a film, the harm done,
checked repeatedly before leaving, secure days,
the cordial afternoons ripe for the bursting,
loving under orders, the attentive misgivings.

The relief on payment, feeling happily foolish,
progress to the next burden, collapsible business,
vanguarded to the hilt, hinting at this space
kissed under orders to an infinite destruction.

Karma blowing up in another face,
security to a fault goes through its motions
foothold in conversation with the guy of games
Tetris on the job, defensive going tout suite.

Working biros now defunct, overworked again,
hedging the bets with impunity, paranoid stance,
a dagger through hearts, dazzling asunder
going into establishments, paying bills so sweet.

Thirsty for sound bytes, counting the cost,
of being off the job for long enough, nicely,
trustworthy calibration in an industrial filter
debts to outer space never killed anybody.

Patricia Walsh

The Credible

From blackboard to whiteboard, a fait accompli,
waiting under orders to a belated sleep,
surely about small money, paid for effort,
wanting to be paid a small feat for the reliable,
daggers awaiting hearts asking for the unworthy.

The illicit threshold, filtered as one knows how,
the bleeding going rate watching-brief in the rain,
already gone postal, your own fault of course,
wrangling out of interest a burning man.

The bilateral supposition never suited anybody,
so get used to you, your grubby paws
on my clean machinery, followed incessantly
ticked off as normal, annoyed as is
the rare possession of self-interested bile.

Once over the counter - it's ours!
the negative hours spent in a licensed hole,
gone to bed for flouting the obvious
the concerned wandering of the schizophrenic lip.

If not mistaken, when?
domestic electricity fails to power without mercy
tight structure gone for pennies, nicely
attention sought and given, covered by depression
the choice opinion, crippled, left in the cold.

Patricia Walsh

Coldly in Love

Wishing for preferment, a recalcitrant prize,
giving headshots where needed, despite protests,
grounds for divorce headed, no hard blankets,
prizes to the lowest bidder lighting the way,
government conspiracies go through another motion,
gone through motions, promised inclusion in same.

seen a world, given an inheritance,
the infinite abuse on the body sought over nought,
driving the fight home, good for the ego,
sidling the mountain, if good, go for the pizza,
promised more than delivered, happy homeless
protesting another abortion, free as maybe.

the steady cigarette burns like a successful fire,
doing another favour in the breakfast air,
the incremental post feeling bitten inside
the portable head hasn't been seen in days
waiting for prizes, not glorying in conversation,
no occupation better than some, glorying a din.

this is our wasteland, nothing more,
relieved over payment being no-one's business,
hard of soft station, thankfully underweight,
other boys, fine, watching for the denouement
going elsewhere for employment, well spoken,
calling before a dinner, greasy though it is.

JAY WAITKUS

Biography

Jay Waitkus is a freelance writer based in South Florida. He has worked as a reporter for numerous publications, including *The Real Daily, The Daily Voice, The South Florida Sun-Sentinel, The Palm Beach Post, The Miami Herald,* and *The South Florida Business Journal.* He is also the author of the crime novels *In the Depths of Shadows* and *Dividing Line,* as well as several short stories and ebooks.

THE DEAD BALL

Julian Williams bounded past the shrubbery encircling Mrs. Altman's yard, hopped his parents' fence, and raced inside through the screen door. Heading straight for the kitchen, he opened the refrigerator, pulled out a bottle of lemonade, and perched himself on the small step stool next to the counter. He looked through the cupboard, retrieved his favorite glass, and filled it to the brim, gulping down the contents without coming up for air. He filled the glass a second time and began drinking again, completely oblivious to his mother, who stood there watching him from the living room with a smile across her face.

"That's a whole gallon," she said. "I hope you're not planning on drinking it all."

Julian laughed as he looked toward her.

"Baseball," he said breathlessly, between three more gulps. "Big game over at Dwyer's Field."

It was early July in Cedars' Grove, and the blazing sun had settled high over the arid, cloudless sky for most of the week.

"Dwyer's Field?" the woman asked. "Is that where you and your brother have been all afternoon?"

"Yep."

"Good Lord, Julian, it must be ninety-five degrees out there."

"Yeah, like I said, baseball weather."

She rolled her eyes.

"Where's David?"

"Still playing."

"Why aren't you?"

"It's hot out there," he said.

"I see."

"We were almost done anyway. And besides, there was something that − something happened, that's all. I just needed a break."

"What happened?"

"It was nothing."

"Julian −"

"It was nothing, I swear."

"Well, good. Then you won't mind telling me about it."

Julian's expression was one of concern, with a hint of trepidation.

"Julian?" his mother beckoned, her normally reserved demeanor now sounding a little strained.

"Nicky got hurt."

"Nicky Figueroa?"

"Uh-huh."

"How? What happened to him?"

"He's fine, don't worry."

"Julian, what happened?"

"It wasn't my fault. It was just an accident, that's all."

"When you were playing?"

"Yeah."

"I think you'd better tell me."

"Aww, Mom."

"Now, please."

"It was no big deal," he insisted. "I was batting, right? Nicky was at shortstop. Mark was pitching. He threw a fastball and I hit it to Nicky."

"And?"

"It was a line drive."

"What's a line drive?"

"See, Mom, you don't even know what I'm talking about."

"Enlighten me."

"A line drive. You know, a ball hit in the air, only real fast and low."

"And you hit one to Nicky?

"Yeah."

"On purpose?"

"No, of course not. I just swung at Mark's pitch. I was trying for a homer. I didn't mean to hit it like that."

"And did he catch it?"

"Not exactly."

"Julian –"

"It hit him in the head."

"Omigod!"

"No, he's fine. I mean, I wasn't sure for a minute. He went down awful hard. But he got up again. He's all-right, honest."

"Did he go home?" she asked.

"Yeah. His mom checked him out. He came back an hour later. She wouldn't let him play anymore today, though. He just sat and watched the rest of the game."

"Is this a normal part of baseball?"

"Well, not usually, but yeah, it can happen."

"Am I safe in assuming your father knows about such things?"

"Well, sure. Dad played in high school, right?"

"Yes, he did."

"Didn't you ever go watch him?"

"I might have caught an inning or two. Sewing club was more my speed. But I never saw anything like what you're describing. I never thought of baseball as all that dangerous."

"It's not dangerous. Nicky's fine. Really."

"Except for the lump on his head."

"Are you gonna ground me?"

"For what? You said it was an accident."

"It was."

"Well, of course I'm not going to ground you," she said. "I may ground your father when he gets home from work, though."

"Can you do that?" the boy asked with a laugh.

"You might be surprised," she said.

"Why would you want to ground Dad?"

"For not telling me how dangerous baseball is."

"You're not going to make us quit, are you?"

"I didn't say that. But clearly it's time I got a little more informed."

"It's just a sandlot game, Mom. It's no big deal."

"Uh-huh. If it's no big deal, why were you so reluctant to tell me what happened?"

"I wanted to tell you. David said I shouldn't."

"Oh, did he now?"

"He said you'd be freaked out."

"He wasn't wrong. I think I'll have a word with him, too. When's he coming back?"

"It shouldn't be too long. They were just starting the top of the ninth. That's —"

"The last inning. That much I know. So, were you winning?"

"David's side was beating us 13-9."

"You're playing against each other?"

"Yeah. Fifth graders versus fourth graders."

"Seems a little unfair for you."

"Why?"

"Well, your brother's a little bigger than you are."

"Not gonna let that stop me," he said. "You know, it's really too bad about that play with Nicky."

"I should say so."

"No, not about him getting hit."

"Julian!"

"No, I mean, of course I didn't want him to get hit. What I meant is, it could have cost us the game."

"Why is that?"

"We had two runners on base. And Nicky never caught the ball."

"Except with his head."

"Right. But that doesn't count. You got to catch it in your glove. It would have been a hit. It could have loaded up the bases. But when he went down, the whole game just stopped. I never ran to first, and no-one fielded the ball. We all just ran over to check on Nicky."

"I would hope so."

"Yeah, but it wrecked the play. Once Nicky got up, we realized it. David said it's called a dead ball. Since we didn't know what would have happened, we did a do-over of my at-bat."

"And did you get on base?"

"No, I popped up to short. That was the last out of the inning. We never got any more runs. At least not that I know of. Unless they're getting some more now."

"Well, finish your lemonade," she said, with a smile. "And go wash up when you're done. You're kind of dusty."

"I slid into home plate in the third."

"I see."

Julian's mother left the room, and he poured himself another glass. He sat down at the kitchen table, sipping slowly now, his thirst finally abating. He was still sitting there half an hour later when his brother walked in, carrying a bat in one hand and a catcher's mitt in the other.

"You left your glove on the bench, Julian," the older boy said, sounding mildly annoyed.

"Sorry."

"Here," David replied, tossing the glove onto the table.

"Is the game over?"

"Yep."

"You won?"

"Don't we always?"

"No."

"Well, today we did. You got one more run, but that was it."

"We'll get you tomorrow."

All of a sudden, though, David's expression turned serious, almost grave.

"What's wrong?"

"Julian, I —"

"What?"

"I'm not sure if there's gonna be any more games."

"Why do you say that?"

"Is Mom around?"

"She went upstairs."

"You didn't tell her about Nicky, did you?"

"Well —"

"You did, didn't you?"

"Yeah," the younger boy conceded. "I told her."

"I knew you would. You shouldn't have said anything, Julian."

"What difference does it make? He's okay."

"That's just it, though. He's not."

"Yes, he is. I saw him come back. He was fine."

"No, Julian. Look, there's no easy way to say this. I wasn't gonna tell you, but I guess you'll find out anyway."

"Tell me what?" Julian demanded.

"We never finished the game."

"But you just said —"

"I didn't know how to tell you this. But I have to, because you're gonna find out. So will Mom and Dad. And the cops are gonna want to talk to you, too."

"Huh?"

"Julian... Nicky's dead."

Julian felt a chill run up his spine.

"What? No! It can't be."

"He was just sitting there watching us. But then he — I don't know, he just collapsed."

"No! You're lying!"

A wave of panic surged through Julian. He looked intensely at his older brother, whose expression remained solemn and mournful.

"You really think I'd lie about something like that?" David asked. "I'm sorry, but it's true."

"Are you sure?" Julian whimpered, as tears began to well up in his eyes.

"I was right there when it happened. He said he still felt a little dizzy. And then he just — he just fell over. We tried to wake him up, but he wasn't moving. And he was cold."

"Omigod. Omigod!"

"Mark and Tommy went to get his mom. But by the time she got there, he was gone. I'm sorry, Julian, but —"

"I killed him!"

"It was an accident."

"But it was my fault!"

"It wasn't anybody's fault."

RON TORRENCE

Biography

Ron Torrence published his first short story at age 50 and his first poem at age 80. Even so his fiction, non fiction and poetry is pretty widely published. He's also written five novels and a screen play, all unpublished. Much more to do. His literary work has appeared in *American Writer's Review*, *Crack The Spine*, *The Dirty Goat*, *Dos Passos Review*, *Existere Journal*, *Forge*, *The MacGuffin*, *Menda City Review*, *Nassau Review*, *riverSedge*, *Orange Willow Review*, *Slipstream*, *Gypsy Blood Review*, *Eureka Literary Magazine*, *Oxalis*, *Ash*, *Potent Aphrodisiac*, *Rockhurst Review*, *The Tower Journal*, *Thereby Hangs A Tale*, *Typo*, *Sour Grapes*, *Circuit Traces*, *RE:AL*, *Reflections Literary Journal*, *way station magazine*, *West Wind Review*, *Wild Violet*, *Menda City Review*, *Yellow Mama*, and *Pleasant Living*.

Ron Torrence

the other side of time

beautiful alicia
always
at the center

penny
small   hesitant   afraid
nobody noticed

alicia
soared
toward stars
she was born to

penny
pushed
pushed
pushed
against degradation
she was born to

in the end

alicia's star
just
beyond
her reach

penny
discovered
pathways
to liberation

alicia jumped

Ron Torrence

from her window
despair

for penny
each step
up the staircase

no matter

how slight

was

victory

Ron Torrence

the curvature of knowing

i
sought
to be the sun

raising mornings
with strands
of gold

bursting into illumination

warming

nourishing

energizing

i became blinded
by light

the valley whispered

come

i
descended
to night shadows

searched pathways
dimly seen

one

to another

to another

interconnecting

Ron Torrence

at the center

illuminated

luminous

moon

Ron Torrence

sisyphus now

hope
rolled her stone
up

great wars
scuppered
her sons' blood

hope
rolled her stone
up

white robed priests
hung
her black children

hope
rolled her stone
up

goose step assassins
incinerated
her people

hope
rolled her stone
up

marauding soldiers
raped
her daughters

hope

rolled

her

stone

up

Ron Torrence

manifest destiny

four helicopters
your apocalypse

blood soaked trenches
my despair

summon my armies
philosophers

sing my songs
poets

paint my skies
artists

your boots
trample
my barricades

you pile
my eye socket skulls
your crypts
all roads lead to

remnants

glory
greece

grandeur
rome

liberty

america

Ron Torrence

quintessence unborn

the gorilla
gazed
at me

wanting to know
what i know

wanting to feel
what i feel

wanting to understand
what i understand

to
walk
away
beside
me

i gazed back

curious

on remembering

haunted

by

her

eyes

SANDY STUCKLESS

Biography

Sandy Stuckless writes in fantasy, sci-fi, and a little paranormal. He enjoys outdoorsy stuff like camping, hiking, and throwing snowballs at his kids. He lives with his family in Toronto.

To learn more about Sandy and his work, connect with him at:

Twitter: www.twitter.com/SandyRStuckless

Facebook: https://www.facebook.com/SandyRStuckless

Fear the Moon

Olarid moved towards the rickety chest on the near side of the single bed to set up his pages, ink pots, and quills. Other than the small table on the other side, it was the only spot he could comfortably work.

"Not there," the man lying on the bed said, holding up his hand. The man picked up a small vial containing what looked like a few shards of silver. There were other oddities on the chest. A still-sealed bottle of lady's perfume, a broken pipe, and a dented flask.

Olarid moved around the bed to the table, wondering if they had something to do with the story he was about to hear. "Shall we begin? I promise to be as efficient as possible."

Orange flame from the wall sconces flickered, creating dancing shadows like a silhouette cabaret. Olarid stifled a yawn behind the back of his hand and shot a quick glance out the darkened window. He should be home in bed with a good book, but the man was adamant about meeting after nightfall. Apparently, paranoia came with old age and from what he gathered of this man, he was extremely old.

Olarid had almost refused the summons, but his curiosity got the better of him when the note promised answers to questions he'd had for a long time.

The third person in the room, a nurse, poured a cup of water in preparation for the upcoming oration. "Are you sure you want to go through with this, Bronwin? The last person to ask for your story left with a limp."

Bronwin glared up at the nurse. "I told you before. He wasn't looking for my story. He was looking to make sure my story never got told."

"So you say," the nurse barked, crossing her arms, "but you nearly killed him."

"I am an old man now, Vera," Bronwin snapped back. "There is nothing to fear from me, but the ones who tried before are still out there. This needs to be recorded before it is lost to my grave with me."

Olarid paused in his preparation. "You sound as if you believe danger is coming."

Bronwin nodded slightly. "It might very well be, scribe. It might very well be."

Olarid pulled a sheet of parchment in close and picked up a fresh quill. "Would you care to elaborate?"

Bronwin stared at the tattered chest with the strange items on it. "There is another supermoon coming and not everyone wants to be cured."

Olarid jotted a few notes, being sure to capture the old man's frail form in words. "What do they want?"

Bronwin grunted as if the answer should be obvious. "Control. To make everybody like them."

"Why not tell your story sooner?" Olarid asked as he sprinkled drying sand onto the wet ink. "It seems a long time to wait."

"It wouldn't have mattered. The supermoon is the key."

Olarid pressed his fingers against his eyes, eager for the old man to get on with it. He was tired and wanted his bed. "How? What do you mean?"

"Patience, scribe. All of your questions will be answered." A fit of coughing took Bronwin as he eyed the cup of water Vera was handing him. "You have nothing stronger?"

"Strong drink is the last thing you need," the nurse chided with a wagging finger, right before brushing a wisp of gray hair from his eyes. "I don't care what you say. There is still some beast lurking within you. I'll not be having it loose in my hostel."

Bronwin pushed himself farther up in the bed pointedly ignoring Vera. She grunted and stalked from the room, chin thrust into the air. Olarid suspected she wasn't that offended, though. The two seemed to have an unspoken understanding.

Olarid froze as the sheet dropped away, revealing telltale circular scars on Bronwin's chest. "I see your eyes on my wounds, scribe. It is time I tell you about the ones you cannot see..."

I knew it was coming. Steeled myself for its eventuality. But as I stared out over my second-floor balcony at the great orange moon, the prison with no door, hovering over the horizon, I realized how sorely unprepared I was for it.

If this had been like any other full moon, I might not have been so terrified. But it wasn't. There had never been a full moon like this. Humans called it a 'supermoon lunar eclipse'. I called it a nightmare.

I gazed across the river as I sipped my amber painkiller, though it hadn't been helping much lately. The soft twinkle of the streetlamps reflected upon the glassy water, while the cool evening mist mixed with the scent of wildflowers and wood smoke. Swirling winds occasionally brought the whiff of drying fish nets. I welcomed them all. They reminded me of what it was to be human. Humanity that was already ripping away like a wound tearing open, spilling fresh blood.

Houses, many of them needing new windows and a fresh coat of paint, lined both sides of the river. All filled with simple village folk carrying on with their joyous and uplifting lives. They laughed and celebrated, oblivious to the monster that lived among them. I wept for them. Death was not even the worst that could happen. It would be a far greater tragedy if I bit them. Unfortunately for them, there was nothing I could do to stop it.

The beast was coming, crashing against me like a tsunami against the shore. The man would be washed away. Fear shivered from my shoulders down through my legs. After every change, the man always returned. I feared after this change, I would never return.

I finished my Scotch while I still could, fighting the growing tremble in my hands. The exquisite liquor warmed my throat, but that fire would be like a candle's flame compared to the inferno about to burst from within me.

Inside the small boarding house room that had been my home for the past four months, a battered and faded chest containing my few meager belongings sat in the corner, propped open with a book. An old table took much of the remaining space with even older books on it opened and useless. Scrolls and sheets of parchment lay strewn all over the floor. None of it useful.

Nothing in all of my readings pointed a way to salvation. Every tome, every scroll, every handwritten note. All useless. There were warnings about this very night, dates scribbled in the margins, and a family descended of werewolf hunters. A mere footnote about a small glimmer of hope. If they couldn't help me... I couldn't go on like this.

Other creatures like me either laughed at the hopelessness – or cried. None could give me any reason to believe in miracles. Why should they? They didn't believe themselves. None could give me a cure.

Some of them wanted nothing to do with a cure. They liked the monsters they were. God knew why. They chased me away when I asked questions and I was convinced they had followed me here. They were as determined to see the cure remain a mystery as I was to see it revealed.

I remembered her, my sole reason for seeking a cure in the first place. Midnight black hair that glistened and curled into tiny ringlets just above her shoulders. Her bright, beautiful smile lighting up even the darkest of days. I could see her plainly in my mind as if she stood right next to me. I wished she stood next to me.

Anna. My Anna…

The tumbler smashed as I threw it against the wall. Even the Scotch couldn't dull the memories this time. Admittedly, it hadn't for some time now. Even if I managed to find a cure, her name would forever be chiseled on that headstone.

Pain like I'd never felt before coursed through my body as muscles contracted. Twisting and ripping, like a jagged arrow pulled from flesh. It was almost time.

I should've searched for escape, as I normally did when the urges struck. Thick woods on the far side of the river, past the houses, stretched for miles beyond. I should already be there. But the cure was supposed to be here, not there. And what of the interloper, another lycan? Would he try to steal it? Still, if something didn't present itself soon, I'd have to make a decision. Escape or murder.

I growled, low and feral as the power of the change seized me. My knees buckled. I couldn't stop it. Oh lord, how I tried to stop it. Every cycle for the past two years, it took me. Two years and countless villages since my hell began. I hardly remembered their names, their faces.

It didn't matter where I went. The curse always found me. Neither the highest mountain nor the deepest cave could hide me. A part of me didn't want to hide. I needed the human contact, the laughter, the smell of cigars and fine scotch, the intelligent conversation. I enjoyed being a man.

My strength grew as I gripped the wrought iron rail. Muscles stretched and tore as the monster rose from the depths. Humanity slipped away. I tried to look away from the giant orange curse, but I couldn't. Its intoxicating gaze lured me in. Soon, the night would be shattered. Blood would flow. Tears would fall.

I couldn't stay here any longer. But two years of tireless work sat inside that small room. As hopeless as it seemed, it was all I had. Perhaps there was a passage I misunderstood, a person I overlooked who could help me. I slammed my fist on the balcony floor. The cure had to be here. I just needed more time.

The pain came again, and with it, an arousal. Like I was the submissive in some sick pact with evil. I wished I could stop it, but I was bound and there was no safe word.

My vision swam. There was no more time. The text said here, tonight. If I didn't find the answer now... I couldn't, no, I wouldn't spend the rest of my days with this curse. Perhaps that was the answer. Tonight would be the end, one way or the other.

Another howl shattered the night's silence. My hunter. He was here. I had to protect the villagers from us both.

I struggled to my feet and leapt--no, fell--to the ground below. A fall that would've been fatal to a normal human. I regained my feet and sprinted into the icy river. The shock of the cold stole my breath for a moment, but it quickly passed as the urge to flee built within me. I sliced through the water like a knife through tender flesh.

I crossed the river in mere minutes and lay on the bank amongst the drying fish nets, ever-sharpening ears catching the quieting laughter. The stink of fear, of piss and sweat, grew stronger. They knew.

As if with a mind of their own, my legs started towards them. One step. Then another. It would be so easy to give in to the urges, to go to them and tear them, rend their limbs from their bodies. It wasn't the joy of pain that drew me to them. It was the scent of their blood. Such sweet liquor...

I forced my feet, against every fiber of my being, to turn north towards the woods. There weren't many houses that way. That was my only chance at salvation. Their only chance.

Keeping out of the glow of the streetlamps, I sprinted by another boarding house. Three stories of brown brick and glass holding all that flesh inside. The scent only heightened the hunger. So fresh. So tender. I could almost feel the raw meat sliding through my claws. I turned towards it, the compulsion too much.

No! I mustn't. I have to fight it.

But I could not turn away. Please, God, help me turn away. I stopped as my disfigured hand reached for the door handle. By sheer will, I forced myself to resist. I just needed to hold on a little long... arrrrrrhhhhhhh!

Clutching the side of my head, I stumbled away from the building. The path to the woods was only a little farther down the road. I was almost there. Almost free.

A man emerged from the shadows near the end of the lane. At first, I thought it might be the other one, but dismissed it quickly. This one walked without direction, without purpose. He stopped for a moment to light his pipe before continuing on. No, no, no, I pleaded. Couldn't you have stayed inside a few more minutes? Damn you and your desire for an evening stroll and a smoke.

A wisp of pungent gray curling up from the pipe bowl somehow seemed familiar to me. As he drew closer, I saw his face clearly. I knew this man. He'd been kind to me, even greeted me those few months ago when I first arrived. We shared a drink on occasion.

I pushed past the stench of the tobacco to savor the scent of his innocent flesh, like a bottle of merlot right when the cork pops out. They always smelled better when there was no fear.

Spinning away from the man, I sought a place to hide until he passed, but no matter which way I went, I would be revealed.

His eyes went wide when he saw me. The pipe toppled from his lips and fell to the ground. On instinct alone, my paw, with razor-like talons, shot out. I couldn't stop it. Like watching outside my body, I was unable to exert any will at all over my limbs. Powerless in every sense of the word. One brutal stroke ended my friend's life before he took his next breath.

My heart wailed as I fought the losing battle to keep the beast contained. How many more had to die by my hand before the end? If I could have torn out my own throat, I would have. The wretched beast within me was too strong. Its will to live was far stronger than my will to die. My existence was nothing but pain.

Staring down into his lifeless eyes, I wondered if he saw me from the other side of the Great Barrier. Please forgive me, my friend.

I wanted to run, to hide, but as I looked back towards my small abode, I wanted to return there. One more look through the papers. One last chance at a bit of hope.

I tore myself away from the body and the pool of blood spreading beneath it. The longer I lingered, the harder it was to resist desecrating the body even further.

I took a few leaping steps towards my room, but then I stopped, indecision slamming into me from all sides. Why couldn't the answers be obvious? Why couldn't they just show me what I had to do?

My head whipped like a pendulum between the woods and the town square. One held their safety, while the other held my salvation. Again, I moved towards the square, past the houses and manicured lawns. The answer was there. I just had to find it.

Their sweet aroma reached my nose before I saw them. A woman and child sauntering down the avenue towards me, so easy, so vulnerable…. What were they thinking? They had to have seen the moon. Did they not realize that the monsters lurking in the shadows were real?

I bolted back towards the boarding house, hoping the shadows would hide me. They laughed and talked without a care. That changed when they saw the smoking man's corpse in the middle of the road.

"What is that, mama?" the child asked.

The mother hesitated, not wishing to confirm the grisly sight before them. "Avert your eyes, child. You need not trouble yourself with such things. Come, I must inform the constabulary."

When they turned back towards the square, I was there, fanged face visible at the edge of the lamp light. I reached out to strike. Such easy prey. The woman screamed and clasped her hand over her mouth. She stepped back slowly, shielding the young girl behind her. I matched them step for step bringing my hideous figure further into the light.

The child whimpered as I let their scent fill me. Citrus and rose. My clawed hand froze, gnarled fingers curling into a tight fist. I knew those scents. They had been Anna's favorite. She wore them the day we met.

But that was a lifetime ago…long before the nightmare. I took another step forward, ever threatening.

The stranger fixed wide, terrified eyes on me, but it was not the stranger's face I saw. Anna's smooth, cream-colored face stared back at me, her eyes sympathetic and forgiving. The small bit of human left in me wailed in agony. Snarling, I pulled my claws back. She may forgive me, but I would never forgive myself. With every ounce of willpower I had left, I stepped back into the shadows.

The woman swept her child into her arms and ran back towards the town square. I did not stop them.

"Anna...I'm sorry."

Olarid lifted his head at the quiver in Bronwin's voice. The pain this man felt for his lost love was strong, still festering, a wound refusing to heal.

Olarid put the black-tipped quill down next to the freshly filled pages and rubbed the tension from his hand. A glance at the hourglass said he'd been writing for almost the full hour. It felt like mere minutes. He poured a cup of water and handed it to a grateful Bronwin. "Would you care for a rest? You have been speaking for a while."

Bronwin lowered the cup and sighed. "No, let us finish this and be done with it."

"Bronwin," Vera warned. "Perhaps you should take some rest. I don't want to see you overdo it."

Olarid couldn't tell if her tone was more wifely or motherly. Either way, it was obvious the nurse cared deeply for Bronwin.

"Damn it, woman," Bronwin spat. "This cannot wait. It is too important." He set the cup down on the table and fixed his gaze on Olarid. "Are you ready to continue, scribe?"

Olarid nodded and picked up his quill.

***

I pushed Anna from my mind and focused on surviving the night. It shouldn't have been hard. I was faster and stronger than them. They were helpless. Except, as I would learn, they were not.

Again, the silence was broken by the howl of the other one. Closer this time. There was no doubt now what his intentions were. He wanted to stop me from acquiring the cure.

The howl came from the far side of the village. If I wanted to stop this lycan, this interloper from ending my last hope, I had to go through the villagers. They would not survive even one of us among them.

It was a chance I had to take to protect the cure. I bolted towards the town square, trying my damnedest to stay in the shadows. Thankfully, the howls had sent most of the villagers inside.

I stopped at the edge of the village square. The gazebo and the manicured grass surrounding it where I pictured many a wedding and other blessings taking place was eerily empty. I didn't know if I should be thankful or worried. Perhaps I was a bit of both.

I looked past the gazebo to the alley between shops on the far side and spotted him right away. Beady, blood-red eyes narrowed, focused in my direction. He saw me too.

My teeth bared and a growl rose from my belly like lava from a volcano. I erupted into action, across the square towards the gazebo. The interloper sprung as well, and we met in the street. His great maw snapped closed inches from my ear, and I caught a rancid draft of his breath.

Powerful fists hammered into my chest as if it were an anvil and I staggered back. This was real pain. For the first time in this form, I felt real pain.

The interloper came at me again, but I stepped aside, out of the reach of his vicious blows. I managed to land one of my own on his jaw, spinning him to the ground. He regained his feet quickly, but I did not give him the opportunity to continue his attack.

My assault was relentless as I clawed at the interloper and snapped at him with my powerful jaws. Clumps of fur and blood flung into the air as we tore at each other.

I could understand it. How the power and strength of being the ultimate predator made them embrace the beast within them. Nothing could stop them. But the price paid was too much. I'd paid too much already.

Grabbing the interloper by the chest, I spun him, sending him cartwheeling through the air. He crashed through the gazebo, splintering the lacquered wood.

Any notion that the lycan was gravely injured fled when he climbed back to his feet and dashed off into the night towards the river.

At first, I questioned why he fled. He was at least my equal, if not my better. He could have beaten me. But then I remembered his goal. He only had to keep me from finding the cure until dawn, when it would be lost forever. The interloper wanted me to chase him.

I had no choice but to oblige him. If I didn't, he would wreak havoc on this village, and I couldn't allow that. Sprinting after him, ground sped by me in huge leaps. I caught sight of the interloper near the split in the road where I had ended the smoking man's life.

He turned back towards me, ready for another round. I stalked in closer, arms spread, ready to defend myself. He stepped towards me and I tensed. One of us would not leave this village alive.

A giant brass bell clanged in the town square. My head spun and I fell, barely feeling the ground when I hit. The bell rang again, and I swore I was being ripped in two. Man torn from beast like meat from bone. The bell rang a third time and I knew. They were coming.

Next to me, the interloper writhed on the ground as well. His agony was equal to my own. I couldn't focus on him. I needed to protect the villagers. Hopefully, the interloper followed me.

Angry shouts replaced the sounds of celebration. A rallying cry. I needed to get away before it was too late. If it wasn't already. The cure was lost to me. I knew that now. It had been foolish to believe such a power could be defeated. My existence would continue until I was lucky enough to meet a hunter's silver bullet. Only then would it be truly over.

Struggling back to my feet, I bolted for the edge of town, towards the darkness. If I could hide there until morning, they might be safe. The sound of the clanging bell followed me, overpowering me.

I was vaguely aware of the interloper running beside me. He wanted to survive as well. If I could do something about that, I would. I would not let him harm the villagers.

They were behind us, chasing us, their voices full of rage. "Stop beast," they shouted. "There is no escape!"

I did not want to believe them. In my mind, I saw pitchforks and torches, but these villagers did not brandish such crude weapons. They had rifles and silver bullets. They meant to kill me. They should kill me. I would be with my Anna again.

But my will to survive defeated my desire for the ultimate freedom. They would not catch me now. I wove between the trees, the whip of the low branches barely registering on my toughened hide. The uneven terrain was no challenge to my gait.

I stopped and sniffed the air. The villagers were closing in. I smelled the sweat on their brows, the gun oil on their rifles. They were determined. A growl of frustration escaped my throat. Why must they persist?

The lycan stood a few paces away growling at me. He turned towards the villagers, death in his eyes. Without thought, I rushed him. Trees and branches snapped like toothpicks as we wrestled on the forest floor. My heart pounded, my breath, shallow. Even in this heightened form, I had only so much strength, so much stamina. I needed to hide.

The voices faded behind us and I thought we had escaped. Then I detected something I had not expected – more villagers, moving towards us from the far side of the woods. The bell, as well as weakening me, was a call to arms. These villagers were cunning.

The first bullet whizzed past my ear, slamming into a nearby tree. Sharp splinters sliced into my elongated nose and thickened fur. Turn around, I begged silently, though I knew they would not.

The interloper ducked under the projectiles as I dashed left and then right. No matter which way I went, they closed in, coming from all sides.

I froze, suddenly aware. If my giant maw could form a grin, it would have. A grin of admiration. The villagers were cleverer than I gave them credit for. It all made sense now. The moon, the bell, the power. It was all connected. The villagers had known all along. This night, this place. They understood the meaning of that moon. They understood the passages in the scrolls. These villagers were my cure. They had prepared for it.

Unlike me.

I knew now that it wouldn't matter which way I ran. They herded us like sheep. There was a sick irony there. Herding the wolf instead of the sheep. Herding the hunter instead of the hunted.

Another bullet struck a nearby tree. Despite my strength, I could not fight them all. I wouldn't fight them. I searched for the interloper and found him crouched behind a wide tree. It gave me a small measure of satisfaction to see him cowering in fear. Now was my chance to end this forever.

I closed the distance between us in a blink and wrapped my arms around him in a powerful bear hug. He struggled against me, but I held the advantage. Time was the only factor now.

The first bullet struck my shoulder an instant before I heard the crack of the rifle. Instead of the momentary sting of it bouncing off my hide, my chest burned as the bullet found flesh underneath. But there was something else. A change.

The interloper convulsed and went limp in my arms. I dropped him to the ground, unable to support him any longer. I tried to move forward but stumbled to one knee. My strength bled from me as red streamed from the bullet wound. I turned to the giant moon and howled. Not out of compulsion, but out of defiance. No longer did its evil grip clutch my heart.

A second bullet hit and again, it did not deflect. I smiled. Darkness lifted from my soul and the man returned. Clear thought replaced primal rage. Now I understood the passages as the villagers did. This moon's curse was also its salvation. None other had the power to break the hold this curse had over me. To live, I must die.

The crackling of leaves under foot told me I was no longer alone. "Begone beast," the stranger's voice commanded, "and leave this man in peace. You are a burden he no longer need carry."

As I collapsed to the ground, I felt only relief. I no longer had to fear the moon.

***

Bronwin's voice trailed into silence and he reached for the cup of water on his table. "Did you get everything?" he asked after a long drink.

"Almost," Olarid replied. "What happened to the other lycan in the forest? Did he become like you?"

"I don't know for sure," Bronwin said with a smirk, "but I suspect he walks with a limp now."

Olarid nodded with a smile. He'd gotten more than he could have ever imagined. Before him was the only man known to be cured of lycanthropy. If the danger arrived as Bronwin predicted, this story would be the only thing that could combat it.

And the opportunity to tell it was his. For years, people had been coming to Bronwin, begging for his recounting of the events. Always he refused. Until now.

A brief word with the nurse explained why. Bronwin was going to meet his Anna again soon. Within days, most likely.

Bronwin grabbed Olarid's wrist. "Be wary, scribe. Those pages may contain mankind's only hope."

"I will guard them with my life," Olarid replied. "You have my word."

With that, he packed his belongings, being gentle with the freshly written pages and retired from the room. It was the last time he ever saw Bronwin, but at least his story would bring hope to others like him.

SHELBY WILSON

Biography

Shelby Wilson writes, teaches, and lives in Amarillo, Texas. He holds a B.A. in English from Texas A&M University and an M.A. in English from West Texas A&M University. His work has appeared in Ink & Nebula, Sparks of Calliope, Backchannels, Celestal Review, Madness Muse Press, and elsewhere.

Shelby Wilson

Thesaurus

I found you in
the back of English classroom 209
in the depths of the cavernous bottom
shelf.

I call you
old (antediluvian, bygone, timeword) and dusty,
despite your claim—
Roget's II: The New Thesaurus.

You advertise:
"Rich in word choices"
on your utile dust jacket.
So why has it been
an eon since someone
has spelunked into
your depths of wealth (fortune, resource, treasure)?

I ply you for a
synonymous rendition
of neglected.
I jam my finger into the
"NP" index notched apse
and begin clumsily thumbing through
your translucent pages.
You confess:
disregarded, ignored, slighted . . . abused.

I remember you
back into the forgotten recess,
only
the forensic and anthropological
evidence of my thumbprint—
to prove that some ancient
being needed you once.

Shelby Wilson

(Almost) A New Yorker

When I book my hotel,
I choose one as far away
as possible from my conference.

I hunger for the commute.
Like hunger for a
bagel schmeared with
lox.

I walk city blocks
in 60 seconds flat
veering around tourists
with heads cocked
skyward in awe of
the concrete jungle.
Messenger bag across
my body in a slash,

I doubletriplecheck
my train,
where I get off,
even which street corner
to emerge back into the bustle,
closest to my destination.

I make sure I
leave my room
with the umbrella
that normally bides
beneath my car seat
back home, jinxing away
the rain that refuses to
fall.

I avoid Starbucks, opting
for local, free-trade,
Manhattan coffee shops,

ordering in the abbreviated
pidgin of hipsters and baristas.
I pop in my earphones,
pretending to ignore
the electricity singing
from the City.

Then, I begin to notice.
My pauses—looking
up at subway signs
when the Natives look down
or stare stalwartly forward,
talking on phones, reading
the Times, the Journal, trade mags.

Their small backpacks
mock my messenger
bag slash, excluding
me from the throng.
Their earphones are
complicatedly threaded
through bags, shirts,
sunglasses, while
mine snag and tangle.

Effortlessness.
I lack the ease,
become paranoid that
the genuine cityfolk
have sussed the lengths
I've gone to assimilate. They've
seen my lot before—
another Almost.

So many Almosts,
they no longer notice how
I want to be them.

Shelby Wilson

English Teacher Pet Peeve #4312 (re:Imagery)

Seeing the phrase "paint a picture," particularly
followed by, at some point, the word "head"
on a student essay makes me want to, well,
I'll illustrate:

Scene opens: atop a suspension bridge.

The cool breeze kisses my face as
the saline smell of the sea below
infiltrates my senses.
The autumnal sun gleams off the
metallic support beams and rails,
dusk imminent.

I begin my sprint toward the end,
the edge,
my legs pumping, teeming with temperate
blood as my muscles go taut and
brace for my leap. The air
rushes past, nipping my ears
with a whispered howl.
Two final flying strides resonate
through my sneakers, the vibrations
are like shivers through my body,
from sole to crown. The sharp edge
of the rail cuts into the ball of my foot
as I hurl myself off the bridge's precipice.

Headfirst and seabound,
the atmosphere roars as gravity's

Shelby Wilson

rush floods my ears. The salty
scent merges with the acidic
bile in my throat.

Skull strikes the water's surface,
electricity shooting from brain to
toes—a quick agony.
The jolt is worth the invited guest—
sweet, sweet Death.

So, I realize my reaction is dramatic, hyperbolic.
My hand scribbles a subpar score and
I move to the next composition.
Dear Lord, it's the offending phrase again.
But they've added the adjective "vivid."
Back to the bridge.

Shelby Wilson

An Execution

Pills clink to the concrete floors
of drug dens across the land—
a crisis, we call it, an overabundance.
This one makes you happy.
This one brings you down.
This one?
It saves her life.
Or it used to.

She sobs in the queue marked
Deathrow Airlines. She edges her
wheelchair toward the plane to nowhere.
Tears in her brown eyes streak
brown cheeks, refracting prismatic
rainbows as the setting sun
floods in floor-to-ceiling windows—
the last glimpse at her life.

Now donning a blindfold, shackled to
her wheelchair in front of the interminable
cinderblock wall,
bullets etched with struck-through
Mercks and Pfizers zip toward her.
Dangling from her hand,
the scales tip and come
crashing down, down.
The bullets clink, clink.
The execution complete.

Shelby Wilson

Dust and Marathons

*"My battery is low . . .
and it is getting dark."*
     - *Mars Rover* Opportunity's *Final Message to Earth*

One day, it all stops.
Cogs, gears, and widgets, caked
with red dust muck will
cease to turn.
LEDs glimmer, fade, and
blink out.
Will memory chips retain evidence
of an opportunity seized or squandered?

From dust, we're molded
by maker's hands,
wound up,
set into motion.
We amble, jog,
are made to sprint
to keep pace,
to live quickly—
no promise of
tomorrow . . .

We comply to the mission,
the control of the race
surrendered to limited resources,
limited parameters,
limited imaginations.

The rare among us
keep

running,
past the tape.
Still sprinting.
The pace transforms into
rhythms of
today,
today,
today.

The rare runs, rolls
from day into night,
through the light
into unexplored darkness—
alone, yet steadfast, singular.

Opportunity is seized
by those created to sprint
who dream of
marathons.

TAMMERA L COOPER

Biography

Tammera Cooper is a self-published Southern author, currently working on the final book of the Water Street Chronicles. She currently lives in North Carolina by the Pamlico River with her fiancé, enjoying their own Happily Ever After. Her own life's challenges inspire her stories of overcoming life's tough patches with love. Follow her writing adventure at www.SouthernRomanceOnThePamlico.com

Tammera L. Cooper

A Sea's Secrets

July 25, 1860, NC coast

The thin, fishbone needle slid through the cotton fabric of the shirt. In out, in out. The sway of the boat tossed the men in their berths. The needle matched its rhythm. His world tilted to one side and then to the other as Abram focused on the ivory point in his boat mate's hand. The hanging lanterns flicked in the dark hold of the sloop. Watching the stitching soothed his want and loneliness. His want for her was strongest after the sun left the horizon. Soon his exhaustion left him with only dreams of her sewing with tiny stitches. Her hands came into focus.

~

Magnolia and jasmine invaded his nose as he leaned on the white picket fence. The sunlight reflected off the small needle case hanging around her neck. Her head bowed as she sewed her handiwork. The needle flowed through the cotton fabric of the small patch she held, and the black curly tendril escaped out of her pins, holding her hair back away from her face. She swiped it out of her eyes. Raising her chin, the light hit the ebony brooch at the neckline of her dress. He closed his eyes and wished for the day that mourning stone would be banished to her jewelry box.

"Hallo, may I join you?" He raised his hand, making a move toward the latch on the gate.

"You, sir, continue to be very forward. Go away." She waved him away and turned back to the cloth in her hands.

"Please, Miss Selah, show me what you are workin' on." He placed his hands back on the top of the fence, watching her continue her work. She pulled out two more patches and ran her fingers across the seams.

"Go away. You wouldn't understand." She raised her eyes. "Why are you here anyway? You should be workin', just like good people do in the middle of the day."

Abram knew she didn't mean anything by it. A pang of guilt ran through him. He didn't take many breaks from his day, but if he could just make her smile.

"Miss Selah, I started my day before the sun. It's not late, but it's been a long day for me. Why don't you come for a walk with me? Just up to the creek and back."

"I'm busy. This needs to be finished before the *Wayward Dawn* sets for South Carolina. I only have a week."

"It's just a blanket." Abram took a step back at the look she gave him as soon as the words left his mouth. "Lands, whoever heard of using a blanket like that in South Carolina anyway."

"For your information, sir, my quilts are famous around the South, and no one will ever sleep under them. They hang on the walls of the largest plantation homes alongside the portraits." She turned back to her work.

"So, send one of the others." He pointed to the quilts hanging on the line.

She shook her head. "No one gets someone else's quilt. The map wouldn't be right." Her hand flew to her mouth as if she had said a curse word. Abram watched as her hands started to shake, and she looked around to see who else was close by.

"Will you just go away? I am busy." A gust of wind blew the laundry on the line so that it was standing straight out, and it snapped like a whip. Abram jumped at the sound and fell out of his bunk, the hard deck bringing him back to the reality of the ship.

The stench of fish and stale saltwater flooded his nostrils, and he knew it had been a dream. He needed to get up top for some fresh air. As he climbed the ladder, the bell started to ring.

"Squall a-comin', squall a-comin'," the lookout yelled from the tall mast above.

Abram skipped a few rungs on the ladder as he hurried to the upper deck. The nets and supplies needed to be secured if the storm was going to be bad, and from the look at the sky, there was no doubt. There were no stars to be seen, and the moonbeams that dared to escape the clouds were few. Abram grabbed a rope and lashed the barrels of precious cargo in canvas before securing them to the side railings.

If it went over, this month would have been all for nothing. "Sound the bell," he yelled to his mate. The young boy left his perch to swing the chain attached to the bell. The deck came to life as the men scrambled to their stations. It was only a small sloop, but Abram would not lose his master's boat and the cargo he had been charged with. The boat took a hard lurch as a wave hit the starboard side. No one stood in one place long enough to feel the steep angle their vessel took.

He watched his crew work, the waves knocking them about. He saw the Yellow Top barrels in the center of the grouping on deck. They sat securely, not shifting with the tide. The maps in the captain's berth showed them close to the Outer Banks, and if this storm had its way, they would join the many on the bottom of the yard.

"We must turn the ship towards the East and go further out to sea." His voice could barely be heard over the water invading their deck.

"But we were headed to port."

"It will only be a delay. To not turn now could mean we lose everything."

His shipmate nodded and grabbed the wheel to turn the boat. The waves crashed against the side, and water flooded the deck as he turned into the wind.

Abram shouted again, "Lower the sails. We will need them once this storm passes." He grabbed the railing just as the ship jolted to port and fell into a great chasm between the ocean waves. He could imagine what Moses felt like walking through the Red Sea. The ocean soon recovered and pushed the sloop up into the air.

He inched across the deck to the cargo barrels and checked their ties. They were tight, but they wouldn't last all night if the crew didn't escape the storm clouds. The sails were finally rolled, but the edges caught the strong wind, snapping back and forth. Lightning crossed the sky, casting a silhouette of Richard tied to the mast. The spyglass faced East.

"Clear skies to the East, Captain."

"How far?"

"A good distance," the man yelled down.

"Everyone, stand fast – we are almost through this." The men remained at their stations. A great wave hit the ship, and it lunged to the port side. Abram watched helplessly as the knot in the rope holding the barrels loosened. The water took five of the barrels over. Abram quickly counted the yellow-topped ones, and a sigh of relief filled his lungs just as another wall of water hit him and sent him toward the grouping. His ribs made a cracking noise as he hit the barrels with all the water's force and his weight. They shifted toward the railing. His eyes opened just in time to see a piece of yellow wood disappear over the side.

Abram inhaled deeply. Sharp pain flooded his right side as he tried to fill his lungs with air. He exhaled, took another great breath, and without thinking followed the barrel over the side. As he dove in, the noise of the storm quieted, and all he could see was the lightning streaking across the surface above him. He swam deeper, spotting the yellow sinking fast. If the barrel had been salt, it would have had a chance of floating. But with its cargo, it would hit bottom quickly.

His lungs started to strain. His breath disappeared, and the pain of his injury pushed his endurance to its limits. He pulled the bowie knife from his belt and pushed toward the barrel. His fingers caught the rough edges of the wooden planks, and he stabbed the small space between the lid and plank, prying the lid open. Great bubbles of air passed his face and raced to the surface. He reached inside and grabbed two small arms curled in front of a small brown face. The small child's eyes were closed tight, but her mouth was opening and shutting as if she was screaming for help. Abram covered the child's mouth with one hand and pushed toward the surface with the other.

The child squirmed in his arms and fought him, but he knew that if he let go, all would be lost. He was almost out of breath. Another streak of lightning lit the surface of the water, and the shadow of the boat above him became his target. He pushed the sea out of his way, pushing toward the surface. His lungs tightened, and the pain in his side dug like a dagger.

The small body in his arms went limp as he broke the surface and started toward the edge of the ship, yelling orders at the figures looking over the side. The crew threw out a rope into the angry sea, and he sprinted toward the loop. He tucked them both in the loop of the hemp and held on. The rope pulled tight as the ocean dropped below them, throwing the ship in the opposite direction. They hung in mid-air only by a lifeline. The oxygen left him as the rope tugged against his ribs.

"Heave ho, heave ho," came the cries of the crew over the wind and rain. A streak of lightning crossed the sky, lighting up the deck. Their bodies slapped against the hull. Water spouted from the little one's mouth as she let out a sputter and then a cough. Abram looked into her wide eyes, trying to reassure her, and then there was nothing.

~

Selah sat under the dogwood tree with her silver needle, sewing in and out of the cotton fabric. His hiding spot in the magnolia tree swayed in the breeze while he watched her through the large leaves.

"I know you're there, Abram." He jerked with her acknowledgment, almost falling out of the tree. "Why do you insist on hanging about? I do not associate with money-hungry pirates. For that is what you are."

"I am an honest fisherman, nothing else," he responded as he pushed the branch and blocked her view. "You have eaten my catch."

"I have seen you unloading the barrels at night from my window. Honest fishermen do not unload their catch by the light of the moon, sir." She turned her eyes down to her work.

"So, you have been watching me at night, have you?"

He watched her pause her handwork at his comment. If her face were not in the shadows of the tree branch, he would have sworn that she was flushed from the conversation. She slowly looked up at him.

"How can one not notice the lanterns blazing at such a late hour?"

"I will tell you of my cargo if you would only come out of that mourning that does you no good. The man has surely faded from your memory by now."

"I do not care about your cargo, and William's memory is as strong as ever."

Her words created a tinge of jealousy that he never felt before. "You are a hard woman, ma'am." He climbed down out of the thick branches and moved across the lawn, moving closer to where she was seated. "But I am unable to stay away from you."

"Sir, you forget yourself. I have no interest in a pirate's company."

"Miss Selah, you mustn't listen to gossips around town. Let me tell you what I really do." He was so close he could smell the rosewater on her skin. Why did it matter what she thought? He wanted her approval. He whispered against her ear, "Let me tell you the truth."

"Fine, tell me then so I will have another reason why I should not take your company."

He grinned and whispered, "The barrels have people in them."

"What? You are a slave trader. I should have known. The only thing worse than a pirate."

Abram shook his head. "No, you don't understand. I…"

"All you care about is money. You, sir, are the worst of the worst, selling your own for profit." She stood up. Moisture from her mouth hit his skin as the words hit their target.

"Miss Selah, you don't understand. I transport cargo, the cargo of friends."

"What?"

"A friend of a friend." He looked into her eyes and saw the understanding as his words sank in.

She looked around the yard and up to the house. "Abram you shouldn't say things like that in the open. Someone will hear."

"But you need to understand – it used to be about the money. I couldn't make enough. I was captain of my master's boat, as much rum and company as I desired. Then I met a young woman traveling in disguise. She paid her own way, bought her own freedom with the blood of finger pricks. Her sewing as beautiful as she, and then I heard of the code in her patchwork. The code that shows the trail to the shore for boats to freedom. I knew on that day that if someone so beautiful could risk so much to help our people, then it was worth it for me as well. The Yellow Top was born."

"The Yellow Top fish I've been hearing about?"

"Aye, the fish."

"So, you sell the barrels to merchants."

"Aye, friendly merchants who transport it north."

Then it happened: she stretched up on her tiptoes and kissed him. A quick smile passed over her lips. Electricity flew through him; he couldn't believe it. The clear day drifted away and became dim. The sun disappeared, and Abram couldn't focus. Everything went dark.

~

His salt-covered skin was tight as he stretched his arms, his ribs complaining and sending sharp pains through his body. Where was he? He tried to focus his eyes, but there wasn't much light. Turning over, pain shot through his abdomen again. There was a lantern swaying from a hook. He was back in his berth, the mustiness from his straw mattress invading his nose. His vision cleared as his hope disappeared. It was only a dream – she doesn't know, she never heard his confession.

The vessel jolted to the starboard side, and he felt the roll of the waves. How long had he been down? And where was his contraband? He tried to maneuver his legs over the side of the mattress, the pain radiating.

"Curses, Richard, Richard," he bellowed. He could hear footsteps scuffing the rungs of the ladder.

"Sir."

"Where is Richard?"

"Captain, he is still tied to the mast, and he says he won't come down until we reach Water Street."

"What? Is he swimmy headed?"

"Perhaps, keeps talking 'bout Yellow Tops."

Abram just shook his head. "How is the ship? Did we suffer any damage?"

"Some torn sails, but not too awful."

The boat tossed to the port side, jostling Abram and shoving him against the back of the berth. He grimaced, grabbing his side and noticing the tight bandages around his chest. "Has the storm passed?" he breathed out, struggling for air.

"Yes, Captain. Just rough seas now. We are headed back into the inlet."

"How are the winds?"

"Full sails, sir. Richard says we will have a pint at The Mulberry tonight." The boy paused. "What about the stowaway?"

"Hmm, what?"

"The stowaway sir. The little girl that you found while you were fighting the Yellow Top."

Abram looked at the boy standing in front of him. He tried to sit up again, but the pain would not allow him.

"What about her?"

"Should we throw her over, sir? 'Tis bad luck to have her here. Richard says it was her that brought on the gale."

"Where is she?" Abram raised his brow, the only muscle that didn't hurt, at his superstitious crew.

"She is sleeping under your desk, sir. Down there." He pointed to the end of the room.

Abram stretched and rolled. A moan escaped his mouth as he caught a glimpse of two small feet sticking out of the gap in the paneling of the desk. "She can stay there until we get to Washington. I will take care of her there." He groaned. "Now leave me and bring me some rum."

"Yes, sir."

~

The ache in his head was dueling it out with the pain in his ribs. He tried to get comfortable but soon gave up. The bindings around his chest allowed little room for him to breathe, but they served their purpose. There was no moonlight or sunlight through the hatch, making it impossible to tell what time it was. He slung his feet over the side of his berth and hollered, "What time is it?" The boat swayed with the waves, but it wasn't as strong as earlier. "I say, what time is it?"

A small voice came from the corner of the room. "'Tis night, and we are almost to port."

It was his stowaway. "And how do you know this?"

She pointed her tiny finger through the port light. "You can see the lanterns."

Abram eased himself off the straw mattress, the sudden effect of gravity pulling on his sides. He let out a groan and grabbed his waist. The small girl ran to his sides, looking up at him.

"What, girl? I don't need your assistance. Get away." She shrank from his reprimand.

His long legs closed the distance to the bow port light to see what she pointed at earlier. It would be no time at all before they made port, where the amber lanterns danced to signal their destination. Then he would have to decide what to do with her. He closed his eyes as his mind wandered with all the possibilities. The Yellow Tops would go to the conductor's station as ordered but now they were one short. What to do? He turned around to look for his tankard of rum. Have a drink, that's what he'll do, and when they get to port, they'll all head to The Mulberry.

~

Clang, clang, clang, clang. The bell rang from the topmast, and Abram stirred in his berth. He planted his feet on the floor and tried to stand, but the pain in his side shot up to his chest, making it hard to breathe. "Ahh," he gasped. He grabbed his cotton shirt and slipped it over his right arm, first tugging at it over his shoulders. He would not offend the women-folk when they docked the ship. He made fast work of the buttons and then pulled himself up the ladder to the deck.

As he poked his head through the hatch, pride filled his aching chest as he watched his crew of five manage the sloop slowly into its slip. The men on the dock already had the nets above the deck, lowering it to be filled with barrels of fish. Arthur, a boy of fourteen, was at the wheel guiding the ship in.

"I couldn't have done it better." He caught the boy's eye and gave him a nod. The ship lightly bumped the dock, and the lad smiled. He continued up the ladder and stepped on deck. "Okay men," he yelled. "Time to get this fish to market. The special order will go on Johnson's wagon." The men moved quickly. The rope was tied around the piling, and the gangplank was balanced. The barrels traveled across the gap in their cradle of hemp to the men waiting on the dock. The drays were soon full, and their catch was on its way to the destination.

The night air blew over Abram, ruffling his shirt. One more stop and he could get some fresh clothes. "I'll meet everyone at The Mulberry. I expect everyone to be there." He glanced up at Richard loosening his bindings to descend from his perch.

"Aye, Captain. We'll beat ya there no doubt."

Abram put his small stowaway on the seat of the wagon, lit the amber lanterns at the corner of the wagon, and climbed aboard. Johnson's wagon was overloaded, and the mule did not want to budge. He gave the animal's rump a slap with the reigns. It just turned and looked at him. A small giggle escaped his companion. He gave him another slap, and the mule reluctantly moved.

"Rum for everyone," he yelled, not remembering the hour. He waved to his crew and set off to Johnson's farm.

~

Spanish moss swayed in the wind and cast shadows on the stone road Abram followed east. The amber lanterns lit the way, only enough for the mule to stay centered in the road.

Slowly, they made their way. The trip wasn't a long one on horseback, but the mule and cart were making it painfully slow. There were torches ahead, and Abram quickly whispered to his companion to hide in the back in between the barrels.

The group of men started to yell as Abram approached. "What are you doing out at dark, negro?"

"I'm delivering fish to the Johnsons. 'Twas a special order and is already delayed."

The man stepped closer to the cart and checked the cargo. "Do you have a pass?"

"Yes, sir." Abram handed his papers to the man as quickly as he could.

"Well, you better make your way. It wouldn't be good to deliver spoiled fish."

"Yes, sir." Abram gave the mule a slap of the reigns, and to his surprise, the mule actually started down the road again without a second slap.

The men yelled a few obscenities as he passed by a makeshift bonfire in the road. Once he was cloaked in darkness again, he patted the seat beside him, and the small girl joined him.

"Watch for the code flowers, girl. The bigger the eye, the bigger the danger."

She nodded her head, and her eyes scanned the sides of the road, moving back and forth. They slowly made their way, and the child pointed to a bunch of black-eyed Susans.

Abram tugged on the reigns and led the mule up the gravel lane to a large barn. He hopped down and opened the barn door. Grabbing the bit at the mule's nose, he backed the cart into the barn. He motioned to the girl to join him, and they both closed the door.

Slowly, they approached the house, the lantern in Abram's hand swaying as they walked.

"You have to go carefully," he whispered so only she could hear.

A light was lit in the kitchen, and the door opened, the wind catching it ever so slightly, so it got away from the occupant of the door jam. Her shawl blew, and she pulled it tighter around her. She raised her candle and waited.

Abram raised his lantern and grabbed the girl's hand, pulling her to the house.

He stayed by the stoop. "Your delivery is in the barn as promised. I'm sorry for the delay. You might want to tend to it quickly. I'm worried about freshness." He winced as the little girl pulled his hand as she hid behind him.

"Who is this?"

"One of the fish escaped, ma'am. I have a net for her."

The woman pulled out a canvas sack that clinked as she moved it. "Your payment sir."

"Not necessary, ma'am. Use it to buy more railroad tickets."

Her eyes widened. He had never turned down gold before, and he knew that she was taken back.

"Just need my horse, ma'am."

"It's behind the barn. Godspeed."

He dipped his head to thank her, swooped up the girl despite the pain, and sprinted across the yard to get his horse. Speed was necessary if he was to hide the girl and get to The Mulberry before his absence was noted.

~

Ale and rum covered the hickory table and sloshed onto the floor, all the men jumping out of the way. The stream of liquid flowed to the edge of the porch and created a fountain to the first floor. Cursing floated in the air with the scent of sweet jasmine, tobacco, and sweat. Abram chuckled as he watched his men unwind after a stressful trip to port. All he desired was the fresh breeze as it blew off the waterfront onto the open porch. The Mulberry was the perfect spot for them to relieve their nervous energy.

"I'm gonna tell you a tale that will shrivel you up the size of a lizard lick."

"A tall tale, no doubt."

"Aye, aye," came the response from the crowd around their table.

"Every word is true." Abram's lookout slung his tankard to the sky and took a swig. "Look at the captain's bindings. Ain't no storm did that. 'Twas the Yellow Top, took him under forty feet at least. I watched from me perch. I never seen anything like it. Lightning shootin' out of its eyes."

The bar wench appeared to clean up the floor that was showering the customers below. "You're feelin' your rum, Richard. Keep it to yourself." She caught Abram's eyes and gave him a demanding look. "You need to control your men, Captain."

"They deserve their fill. We are out of the way. I will see that they cause no trouble."

"They already drank up half my good rum, and now they're startin' on the other. I wouldn't care if half of it wasn't covering my other customers downstairs."

Abram leaned over the railing and gave the men downstairs a wave. "Maybe I should invite them up." He gave her his brightest smile, his white teeth sparkling against his sun-darkened skin.

"Nay, there are enough people up here. You want the pizer ta come down?" She gave him a wink.

Abram laughed and winced, the pain reminding him of his injuries from the previous night.

The tavern wench leaned over, giving him a good view of her ampleness that his men loved. "What really happened last night?"

He slid some doubloons toward her on the table. "There are things best left to the sea."

TAMMY L. BREITWEISER

Biography

Tammy Breitweiser is a writer and teacher who is a force of nature and a conjurer of everyday magic who is always busy writing short stories. Her flash fiction has been published in Spelk, Clover and White, Cabinets of Heed, and Elephants Never. Her essay is in the *I Wrote it Anyway* anthology. You can connect with Tammy through Twitter @TLBREIT.

App World

The metal container groans from the weight of the bodies. The transmission whines loudly as it struggles to shift. A struggle bus... literally.

I am once again pushing the line of late and on time which reminds me of persnickety middle school teacher definitions. Am I in my seat or just in the room to be tardy?

I look out of the window to check the route and see a pink elephant. *Hmmm... that isn't right.* Then I see the black and white circus tent.

I really need to get more sleep. My meds are messing with my brain.

Every day for a year I have written in my journal about my desperation to escape from my life and job. The place I would rather be is a library that contains a kitchen and bathroom.

I am visualizing sitting at the desk in the library my fountain pen moving over my notebook in the sunlight and I start to feel like I am looking at myself from an outside perspective. I used to dream as a child that I was tied with a cord to my body and I could see myself sleeping.

I feel eyes on me and raise my gaze from the floor. The man across the large aisle on the bus facing parallel to my side is staring at me. Hard.

I smile and nod not really knowing what else to do.

Darkness immediately falls across his face and he says, "You shouldn't be able to see me."

Clearly, I do see him, which agitates him more.

He starts to shake and look around wildly,

"Why can you see me?"

My stomach feels like I have been punched. I press the strip to be let off the bus. I don't even know where we are on the route and I don't care. I just need to get off this bus now.

As I exit the metal machine, I see the house I have only seen in my mind's eye for 365 days. What is going on? It cannot be here. I have imagined my life so different over the last year I'm beginning to be a little unnerved about how pieces are manifesting in this place. Words and thoughts have power, but not construction. My stress relief has now created a tangible trouble

I feel like something is off by standing in front of this house from my imagination.

Over the past year, my dreams have gotten very vivid and I've been able to interact with them. I didn't really think anything of it at the time just that I was focusing on the writing so I figured that it was in my mind in my head was coming along I use the dreams to add detail to the journal entries every day about the baseball Diamond and the pink elephants and the circus and the library house and the tiny house that I have that I travel with

I stand on the side of the street looking at the tree-lined driveway when I hear:

"Is that really you?"

The friend I see in my dreams is standing in front of me. She is real. Her crystal blue eyes are the color of the Caribbean ocean and her straight hair is as black as fear. She is athletic, intelligent, and loves to read. In my ideal world journal, we talk about books and writing every day.

"Why are you here? You aren't supposed to be here."

"I don't know. I am so confused. There are buildings and scenes in front of me that are real that have only been written."

"You put it into the universe, and it has manifested itself. Do you have your phone?"

"Yes, why?"

"Let me see it."

I pull it out of my bag but do not hand it over. Everything is a little too weird.

"You have an app on your phone which opens a portal to this world. Your dreams have been seized here. It happened when you were writing on the bus."

I wanted to escape my reality so badly I have now created a new world.

STELLA SAMUEL

Biography

Stella Samuel is a women's fiction author whose credits include her novel *34 Seconds,* her published collection of short stories, *Stories South Of The Sun,* as well as several short fiction pieces published in various literary magazines.

While earning her BFA in Creative Writing for Entertainment from Full Sail University, she developed a children's writing workshop and a publishing company, ARZONO Publishing.

Stella has been an Alliance of Independent Authors member since 2016. She lives in Arizona, a place she calls a mile south of the sun, with her partner Jessica, three children, and a myriad of pets.

Father, Mine and Someone's

He wouldn't have danced with me, my father. The day he gave me away, I told him we were only having dinner, not a full reception. Ours wasn't a traditional wedding anyway, so skipping the father-daughter dance wasn't a big deal to me.

Dancing wasn't the only thing he wouldn't do. He wouldn't have read my screenplays, but he'd happily watch the movies once some Hollywood director ripped apart my words until the idea behind them was all remained. He would laugh though. No matter what we were doing so long as it wasn't dancing, he'd laugh with me. A quiet all-knowing laugh that would leave me wondering if my laugh didn't quite hit the rhythm of the joke. And he'd talk with me.

He'd ask questions, wonder where my life was, where it's going, and what I needed from him to reach my dreams. He'd listen to my complaints. Funny, I don't complain about the same things today as I did then. I wish he knew. I wish he knew me today. I could tell him I am closer to the young woman he used to know. Not the teenager who fought him every step of the way. Not the teenager who'd been raped and feared not the consequences but rather telling her father her secrets. All of them. The small girl who picked clovers and sang the same song wondering if they were red clovers or merely a shade of red along with clovers and the young woman who wanted acceptance, not just tolerance, needed to find a place of warmth in her father's arms again. I was that girl again, not the in-between-girl, while dancing.

But the dance, the journey, began long before. Not in a field of clovers but in sound of the blooms coming out to live free.

***

Honeysuckle sweetened the sour air outside my father's house. Closing my eyes, I inhaled the scent of nectar while twisting the ring I wore on my right hand. Unless he'd seen the headlights from my car rising up through the dust, Dad wasn't aware I was there watching him. His silhouette in the light of dusk only lit up when he inhaled the carcinogens from the cigarette in his left hand. As had been threaded through my childhood and adolescence, music filled the air. Dad had built a wall unit to hold his stereo several years back. The massive stereo, as esteemed as a family heirloom, was the centerpiece of the family room. When we weren't watching the latest Thursday night sitcom, music was on. It was how I'd spent my childhood. From sitting on his lap as a young girl to adulthood struggles, the soundtrack to my life was Dad's music. Irony closed in on me as song lyrics spoke thoughts of loving her. Pursing my lips together, I smirked at the song. Tommy James and the Shondells was a band I'd been singing along to since I could make sounds. This was an album my father listened to again and again. When times were tough, when stress was overwhelming, when sadness took over his emotions, the lights went out, a match struck, and Tommy James sang of love and clovers.

This time was no different. I had run away. Life doesn't allow us to run long or far, but it didn't stop me from trying. I had to get away to find my support. To find myself. The only thing I'd realized from my choice to run was my life wasn't a choice, and I needed to be true.

After spending five days in the hospital with Kris, I'd said my final goodbye. Her death was an awakening to me. Every beat in the song of clovers reminded me of the rhythm of her heart. The one I used to hear with my head on her chest. But only while it still beat. Beneath the tiny feet of squirrels sounded a crunchy autumn of the past, and hanging in the air, the crisp spring scent of honeysuckle mingled with sounds of musical waves leading to me stand in a doorway wondering if I had the strength to tell my father the truth.

"Dad?" The door squeaked as I opened it. A light went on as if his fingers were on the switch waiting for me.

"Hey." It was all he could say to me.

I did call him collect from nine hundred miles away to tell him I was safe. My dependence ran deeper than tolerance.

"You're home."

"I am." Neither of us dove into the conversation we needed to have.

"I'm sorry I left," I said with a cracking voice. "Maybe we can talk?" The question in my tone asked to be Daddy's girl again.

"Are you okay?"

"I am okay. It's been a rough few weeks. Kris…"

Tears fell from my jawline to the floor. I'd hidden too long. I was exhausted from hiding. Afraid of showing my weakness, I sat. The couch fabric scratched my skin as I pushed my body back. With elbows on my knees, I stared at the carpet below. It was a cesspool of dark hues and stains. Yellow light from overhead dulled the browning cigarette smoke laden carpet below my feet and reflected on the cobwebs draping the walls behind my father's chair. Our conversation was about as pleasant as smoke stains seeping from the walls.

"I lost a good friend in a car accident, too. When I was your age, I mean." He was trying. At least he was talking.

"Dad?" My voice cracked each time I said the word. "I've lost everything."

"You have your health. And your job."

"I'm nineteen. Of course, I have my health. And I wouldn't have a job if I were back in school."

"I'm not going to feel guilt for this. You want to go to school, sign up. But study something that will get you a better job than you have now. You need to be in business. Or computers."

"Dad, I love theatre."

"Fine. Study business. Join a theatre. If you can get a job in theatre, great. But you need a backup plan. You need a future."

"I don't want to argue, Dad. I want to tell you about my trip. About me. About what I experienced. About Kris." A tear slipped from my eye, running as fast as I'd run, before soaking into the carpet leaving another dark spot.

"How about you tell me about that tattoo?"

"It's Pop-Pop's guitar."

"You're never going to get a good job with a visible tattoo." His words bit. Word after word, sentence after sentence, the space between us grew larger. There was no way we'd ever find commonality.

The music had changed. The silence built between us as lyrics changed from loving her to new days coming. Change. People changing. I had to keep trying. We had to find that place again. That place where I climbed up onto his lap and wrapped myself into security and everlasting love.

"Kris," I sobbed. "She wasn't just a friend. She was my girlfriend." The words came out faster than my mind could think them.

"What? What do you mean?"

"Dad."

"The tattoo? You got it for her?" He looked closely at my leg. Names surrounded the shiny guitar still covered in healing ointment.

"No. I got the tattoo for me. I play guitar. Music, thanks to you, Dad, lives in my soul."

"She was your girlfriend? You're gay?"

"Yes, Daddy." In my mind, I'd already crawled up onto the lap I remembered as the warmest and loving place in the world.

"Well," Dad said. His eyes didn't leave his father's Gibson Sunburst on my ankle. "We finally have something in common."

"You have a tattoo?"

"No." The silence sang louder than Tommy James. Dad stood, took two steps, and wrapped his arms around me. "I like girls too."

Crimson and Clover played again from the wall speakers.

Over and Over.

***

Now he's gone, my father. But I got to dance. And we laughed. The music blared, disco, then The Temptations, and Sister Sledge. I danced with a man who was not my father. A man who took time to show me steps even my father didn't know.

"I don't know how to two-step," I said bending my neck to view the white hair towering over me.

"It's three steps," he said. "Two to the right, one back."

"Then why is it called two-step?"

"I don't know, but I'll show you how."

I hadn't danced with a man in many years. But we connected. Sure, with the Manhattans for me and an abundance of beer for him, he led me to believe the forty years between us kept him young on that floor.

"Forty years! We don't have forty years between us!" Light above my head dulled as I closed my eyes imagining my twenties as if they were yesterday. I hadn't moved like this since that time.

"Well, I know you're a lot younger than I am, whatever the difference is. You're keeping me young," he said. My body spun into his. I was getting the hang of letting him lead, which wasn't an easy feat.

My wife came over with another drink for me and looked at him with a crooked smile. "Your wife wants to know if you want another one," she said.

"I'm exhausted. Yes, I need another one."

We sat and laughed. His wife was beautiful. And funny. She and my wife connected. But on a different level. In their world, they could be neighbors. Friends.

Another song came on, and we danced. Sometimes all four of us, sometimes just me with him, and for some songs, I stood back with bourbon in my hand watching my wife's body do something it does so well. Her movements like ocean waves. Closer to me, then pulling away leaving me wanting another ride. Between the lights and the music, the bourbon and the elation, I allowed myself peace watching her dance.

"This is our song!" he grabbed my hand, so I could dance another one. We didn't have a song. He barely had a name, at least not in my world. But we had a connection. One that I missed because I hadn't had one like that in the years since the clovers.

For one evening, I connected with someone's father. And remembered mine.

~ ~ ~

I wrote this short in 2018, six years after saying a final goodbye to my father. There will always be a hole in my world where Dad used to live. It's so good to embrace who we are exactly where we are and love those around us. Jessica and I are both blessed years later to have George and his wife, Marie, in our lives after such profound loss.

~ Stella 2020

CHARLES COOPER IV

Biography

Charles is a member of the Class of 2020 headed for High Point University in the Fall. He has been writing for several years now combining the topics of science with ancient history to create stories which provide a dramatic vision of history through the lens of science. He also writes poetry around the same subjects.

Riverside Vigil

The river flows and here I sit.
The river flowed when they called me King.
The river flows and here the King sits.
Here the King sits and here he sees.
Mountains and statues they built.
Mountains and statues for me.
In the mountain they buried me.
"King," they called me.
King of this land.
King in life and King in death.
In the mountain they stole me.
And now the statue I inhabit.

Forty centuries of flow and flood.
Forty centuries of sand and sun.
I see my Kingdom fall.
Once. Twice.
Thrice and frice and fice.

The conquerors from the east.
Those that ruined my face.
Strange symbols from a far place.
Symbols of moon and star.
The conquerors from the west.
Those that leveled the sands.
Strange banners from pale lands.
Banners of red, white, and blue.

The river flows and here I sit.
The world now sees me.
But they do not know me.
Forty centuries.
Now the world sees me.
And I am content.

Forgotten Queen

Why, my nephew?
Am I condemned?

I was your aunt!
Your mentor!
Your Queen!

Your father was a buffoon!
And so I ruled.
While he brought down elephants.
I brought down revolts.
While he was worshipped.
I was consulted.

You were his heir.
You needed to be right.
You needed to be better.
All you did was fight.

I buried your father.
And you were but a child.
I buried my father.
And myself with him.

You were good.
You were a father.
To a monster who hated my every breath.
It was him wasn't it?
Him who took me.
Him who left me on this floor in darkness.

For thirty centuries I sat here.
Next to my nurse.
The only one who cared.
When the strange men entered they took her too.

Again I am abandoned.

Charles Cooper IV

The strange men who left me in darkness.
For a century after I sat here.
And here I will turn to dust.
I know it.

So why, my nephew?
Am I condemned?

There's a noise.
The strange men returned.
They talk in words I do not understand.
They put me in a box.
From the floor I have left.
And I am content.

KIRA METCALFE

Biography

Kira Metcalfe has a degree in English Literature from Ryerson University in Toronto, Canada. Her poetry has been published in White Wall Review as well as several digital literary magazines. Kira works and lives in Toronto.

The Golden Statue

It's Hollywood's biggest night. Polly and her friends clamour around the flat screen, each with a Vanity Fair prediction printable in hand. Everyone ignores the talk of Marchesa and Saint Laurent. Randy stumbles through the door without knocking, a joint hanging from his lips.

"Here comes the fun!" says Randy.

Polly rolls her eyes.

Janet, Paul, and Mark follow Randy inside, all of whom likewise don't appreciate the subtle art of red-carpet coverage. Randy plops onto the loveseat next to Polly.

She promptly turns on her hostess voice. "Shh! It's starting!"

Janet follows the opening monologue with a yawn while Paul and Mark return to discussing the state of American Politics. This ought to be good, thinks Polly.

"Mark, come on. It's the era of Trump. I don't think we even know what that actually means. I do know we're fucked though," says Janet, flicking her cigarette ashes into her empty glass.

Polly pushes the ashtray on the coffee table towards Janet who gives her a thin-lipped smile. In the background the TV blares commercials for an actor-endorsed gin company. Polly stares at the flashing images but gets snapped out of it by Mark and Paul's escalating tones.

"Fuck Trump. Let's get drunk," says Polly.

"That almost rhymed!" says Mark. Randy pokes his head out of the kitchen.

"Don't worry, already on it!"

"Make mine a double," says Janet.

Polly sits back pleased with the glass of Merlot Randy brought her.

To her left Jodie and Ronnie are discussing the repercussions of James Comey's firing last May. She can see Mark wants to get in on their conversation. Janet and Paul are now well into a tête-à-tête regarding the pros and cons of acting in digital projects versus traditional media.

"Yes, ad revenue sucks, but if the channel's tied to an MCN you got some stability there," says Paul.

Polly and Randy give each other a look as Janet pulls Paul off the couch mid-sentence and takes him across the living room to the open balcony door. Janet can only enjoy her alcoholic beverages with a breeze in her hair. With everyone in their resettled positions, Polly and Randy continue debating the gender wage gap.

"People need to tell each other how much they make. Especially in the same industry," says Polly.

"Umm, no! I don't want anyone knowing what I make. It's just gonna cause problems."

Polly cocks her head back with a sly smile.

"What if it got you a raise?" asks Polly.

Randy shifts his eyes back and forth in thought and purses his lips.

"Touché."

Polly takes the last swig of her Merlot. Randy heads to the kitchen but turns around, the wine bottle sitting on the counter a few feet ahead of him.

"But—"

Polly interrupts him, chuckling, "Oh for fuck's sake, at least get my wine first."

Across the room Polly hears Demetri bring up the Best Picture snafu from the year before, answered by a roar of laughter.

Randy brings the bottle of Merlot to the coffee table. As more of the same commercials flash across the screen he tops up Polly's glass, lips flapping with statistics. Even with the volume of her wine glass adequately maintained, Polly checks out of their conversation. She starts wondering how much the ad fees tonight are compared to the Super Bowl. Polly grew up watching the Super Bowl and only started watching the Oscars when she got serious about acting.

Everything is only as important as the money put behind it. She waves her thoughts away, just as she waves away the smoke from Randy's joint.

The room goes still and quiet suddenly, but Polly is certain there's still another half-hour until the last major categories.

"What the fuck!?" says Janet, starring at the TV.

Everyone turns their attention to the show for the first time since it began. The picture is hazy now and screams echo from the speakers. Red and gold opulence is replaced with shrieks and toppled cameras. Within seconds the SMPTE colour bars pop up and the screams are replaced with a high-pitch whine.

Everyone's phones chime with the same chirp of Twitter notifications, creating a melody back dropped by stunned silence mixed with singular words of disbelief.

"Someone on Twitter is saying it was a bomb," says Mark.

Polly's eyes lock with Randy's, both turn their gazes over to the mantel. In the middle sits a golden statue from the year before.

Polly turns to him, "Rand, I was supposed to go."

TAMMY BIRD

Biography

Some people buy a fancy sports car or fly to far away lands when they hit middle age. Tammy started writing fiction with strong female protagonists. A literature professor by trade, she deemed it fitting to write about the kaleidoscopic prisms of human nature in her thriller/suspense stories and novels.

Be warned, her work is psychologically hard and gritty and real. Her second novel, THE BOOK OF PROMISES, a YA suspense set in Denver, CO, is currently available on Amazon.

Appalachian Mountain Girl

You would think being raised on a hog farm, we would be used to the high-pitched squeals of death. Some of us are, sure enough. But I'm not, and neither is Gordy. Gordy's my little brother. Granddaddy says he acts more like a girl than a boy. I don't think that's fair. For one thing, not all boys wanna cut things up. For another, girls ain't always afraid. I'm not. I don't like the sounds, but I ain't scared. I pretend to be for Gordy. He's only ten. He needs somebody on his side.

"Two peas in a pod," my momma says. I see her feet coming toward the bed. She's here to coax us out. "Come on, you two." Her worn out slippers poke into the dark. "It's over."

I've never actually seen the slaughter. I don't have to. I'm a girl. Momma says our job is getting things ready in the house. I'm happy about that most days, but sad for Gordy. He's in the last year he gets to choose. He was supposed to choose on his tenth birthday, but daddy said he wasn't advanced enough, said he needed one more year. My granddaddy said a lot of bad words that day. It messed up Gordy's birthday real bad, especially because my daddy left that day and never came back.

"Bess," Momma says, "take your brother's hand. Don't make me come after you."

Gordy is in a ball under the bed. When I reach for him, he pushes deeper into the corner like he's trying to disappear into the worn wood. It doesn't work. If it did, I would gladly follow him. A dark abyss would be heavenly darkness. "Take my hand, Gordy."

I feel his cold fingertips first. They shake against the back of my hand. I turn my palm up and slide my fingers between his. "It's okay. We'll do it together." I give a gentle tug.

"Bess!" There is no patience left in momma's voice.

Bile nips at the back of my throat. "We're coming, momma." I hold on tight and tug fast and hard, like I would to pull off a band-aid. We slide into the light.

"Make yourselves useful," Momma says when we finally get to our feet. "Your granddaddy and brothers will be here soon, and they're gonna need a bath."

"Yes, ma'am."

I don't let go of Gordy's hand as we head to the well. I'm fourteen. It's my responsibility to keep him safe, and I know from experience that if he doesn't absorb the smell of blood while I hold tight, it will spook him, and he will run. It wasn't like that before Daddy made him go to the barn the day he turned ten. Whatever happened in that locked up old barn wasn't good for either of them, cause Daddy's gone, and Gordy isn't a carefree little boy anymore. In fact, he ain't like a little boy at all except the scared part. "You okay, little brother?"

"I never want to get in the red-stained tub." His voice was barely above a little-boy whisper, but the conviction was strong like a man.

I think about the big silver tub in front of the pot belly stove. Granddaddy will wash first. Then Junior. Then Clarence. I want to lie to him, but I can't. "I can't promise that, Gordy."

When his time comes, he will wash last.

"Can't we leave? I mean you and me?" Gordy asks.

I realize his hand is no longer in mine. He pivots. We are face-to-face. It's the first time I realize how tall he's grown. I don't answer. I just start moving again toward the well.

That night, Gordy slept with me.

As he fell into a deep sleep, I felt his steady breathing turn into quiet whimpers. He should be dreaming of playing chase on the mountainside or about sitting in class learning arithmetic. But his dreams are nightmares about his place in the family business, about his grace year coming to an end. They always are.

I drift into my own nightmare thinking about the sounds and smells of the day. Part of me wants to take my rightful place in the business. I ain't no scared little girl. I can slaughter same as a boy. But granddaddy says no. He says girls are girls and boys are boys.

Sometime during the night, I hear it—a thud from below the loft. At first, I think it is the dream, but it comes again and again. I slither out of bed and over to the loft railing.

Granddaddy's large calloused hands are around my momma's neck, and he is pounding her against the wall. I watch in silence as her feet swing out wildly. At first, I think she's fighting, but the movements are erratic, like she isn't really there at all. Her lips are moving too fast to read them. I rub my eyes to clear them of the darkness behind me. I need to read what they are saying.

"This business feeds you." Granddaddy says in a low growl. "You will not tell me who will and who won't be a part of it. You understand?"

Momma's lips move more slowly. They mouth, "He can't do it."

The *he* must be Gordy. I hate that Momma is hanging like that, but a little smile comes out anyway. Maybe Gordy won't have to wash in the blood-ringed tub.

My happiness is ripped away a second later when Momma drops like a rock to the floor and curls into a tight circle.

When Granddaddy's steel-toed boot makes contact dead center mass with the lump that is my momma, I feel it in my gut. The gasp that escapes me sounds loud in my own ears, but momma's own groan covers the sound. Granddaddy's eyes never move from Momma's body as it lurches up in pain and then moves across the floor like a balloon losing air.

"I need more hands," Granddaddy says. "Business is pickin' up, and it's that sniffling kid's fault I ain't got his daddy no more."

Granddaddy moves in slow motion until he's above Momma again. "Get up. Get him up. It's time he does the day-after chores with me."

Momma is holding her stomach, but she still stays quiet. At fourteen, I realize she's doin' it so we kids don't hear. I wonder if this is part of bein' a girl.

"What about the boys? Let them do it." Momma's voice is soft, but I don't have to read her lips anymore. I can hear the words. "Or let me. I can do it. We can go now."

"You?" Granddaddy laughs out loud.

I swallow hard, try to be quiet like momma.

Granddaddy's boot comes up and then down hard on Momma's throat. "You can't barely clean the tub after, you dumb broad. How you gonna slice anything open?"

"I'll do it, Granddaddy." I didn't know I was gonna say it 'til I did. But it's my job to protect Gordy. Now it's my job to protect Momma, too.

The smile that came on Granddaddy's face sent a chill right through my nightclothes.

"Well. Well. I knew you had it in you. More like me than your momma and daddy believed."

"Yes, sir." It was all I could think to say.

"You're still a girl." Granddaddy looked down at momma. We both knew cause we knew granddaddy that he was tryin' to decide about beliefs and business.

I stood tall at the edge of the rail and met his eyes like I saw my older brothers do when they talked about the business. "You need me to do it. I ain't afraid like Gordy. Gordy'd just slow you down."

"Get on in there and get dressed," Granddaddy said. He moved his boot offa momma's throat. "We have work to do."

Momma mouthed, "Thank you," right before she rolled from under his shadow and I turned to go back to my room. I'm not sure if it was for Gordy or for herself. Probably both.

All three of my brothers slept through the commotion. Thank goodness for that. If I was going to do this, it needed to be just me and Granddaddy.

I still don't know what time it is when we make our way to the barn, but the dark is still low to the ground, and the thick air is still consuming all sound. We don't speak until we reach the big wooden doors.

"You ain't gonna puke on me, are you?" Granddaddy asked while he turned the little silver key in the lock.

"No, sir. I ain't gonna puke." I didn't either. When those doors opened, and the smell hit me straight on, I squared my shoulders and walked right in. I remembered Daddy telling my brothers that the hardest part was facing it for the first time, but after you faced it, it wasn't so hard. Daddy was right. Momma was right, too. Gordy couldn't do this.

"Come sit next to me, Bess. I'm gonna explain the tools and how we use 'em. You have to be safe when you work."

I thought he was gonna say, 'Specially since you're a girl,' but he didn't. I was happy about that.

For the next hour I listen and learn. It is all quite fascinating in a family business kind of way.

"You aren't so strong, yet," Granddaddy said at the end of my first lesson. "I'll have to do the hard work. You'll learn. And those scrawny girl arms will grow each time we have a job to do."

I believe him. When I pick up a small tool with a round head, a warmth spreads through my body. "Does this cut through everything, Granddaddy?"

"That's an autopsy bone saw. What did I tell you about that one?"

Our eyes meet. I see only tenderness. I feel all prism-like in my tummy. I belong here, and he has accepted me. "The blade oscillates. It doesn't grab." I put the blade against the carcass and push while I answer, then I turn it over in my hand. "It isn't heavy."

"It will wear your arms out just the same." His smile is genuine—not like the smile he gave my momma. "It suits you."

I nod and turn the tool over in my hands again and again. The smell of blood isn't as strong now. "Can I try it?"

"Patience. Remember, it will only jiggle the skin. I have work to do before you begin."

"Granddaddy?"

"Yeah?"

"Do you like having me here?"

"More than I thought, for sure."

"Granddaddy?"

"Yeah?"

"I'm gonna make you proud."

While I watch my granddaddy work, I think about Gordy. I need to make Granddaddy promise...

"Come here." Granddaddy's words cut into my thoughts.

My heart is racing when I reach his side. It is my turn. I'm a genuine part of the business, now.

I don't even notice the sun peeking up until every last piece of meat and bone is placed into buckets. "What do we do with it?" I push a strand of hair out of my face with my arm.

Granddaddy's hand squeezes my shoulder. "It's time to feed the hogs."

I nod. He was right about my arms. They feel like they are going to fall off my body. I don't wanna change his mind about a girl in the business, though, so I pick up two full buckets and head out of the barn. We need to work quickly.

Walking back to the house, Granddaddy tells me I did about as good as my brothers on their first time. He also tells me about the man who hired him to do the job we just finished. "We are in the business of making people disappear, Bess. We've been doing it for generations. Our client found me by word of mouth. None of that fancy technology that's going around. They pay half up front and half when we finish."

It sounds weird to hear my granddaddy use the word client. I know what it means from school, but he didn't go to formal school. "You have a lot of clients."

Granddaddy nods. "Cause people know they can trust me, Bess. That's what you gotta remember 'bout our business."

"But why did he want that man dead?"

"That ain't none of our business. Best you don't ask questions. This could be your business one day. Somebody tells somebody else. They pay. We deliver. The hogs eat good. No more. No less."

"Yes sir."

"We'll get cleaned up now. I'll send those lazy brothers of yours to the barn to finish the clean-up. You'll sleep. You deserve it. You did good work today."

"What about you, Granddaddy? Will you sleep?"

"Not yet. First I'll go to town to get word to my client."

My eyes hurt. Actually, everything hurts, but Granddaddy says I did good today and Gordy doesn't have to be a part of the business. As long as I keep learning, Granddaddy will keep that deal.

When we reach the house, Granddaddy looks at my momma. "Let her get in first. She earned it. She's better than any of them boys combined."

I have a lot more to learn, but while I sit in that scalding hot water and watch my fingers get the prune-like ridges, I know that I'm where I am supposed to be. Granddaddy said it—I'm better at this than any of them boys combined.

ACKNOWLEDGMENTS

Stella Samuel

First and foremost, I'd like to thank and acknowledge my life partner, my love, my partner in parenting, cooking, silly voices, and laughter, Jessica, for providing unfaltering, never ending support to me and the time it takes me to write, publish, and help others meet their dreams of making a difference with words. Since Will and Nikki and a short pause in a parking lot, I have loved and appreciated you and everything you give to me. I thank my children for efforts of understanding and for constant hugs and tender moments.

Charles Cooper, when I came to you almost two years ago with an idea to uplift writers and build a place to nurture a tribe, I never imagined it would take me this long to develop such a world. Thank you for your patience in me and the trust we could do something cool for others.

I'd also like to acknowledge a few people I'm going to lump together in one large group. These people are support, love, kindness, the belief in myself in moments I stop believing, mentors, and friends. Thank you all for being a part of my tribe. Courtney Ruedisueli, Anne Mellichampe, Elizabeth Saunders, Nick & Christy Nocero, Ken & Allison Moskowitz, Romall Smith, Kasisi Harris, Joan McHugh, Penny Reedy, and my mother, Marlene Rennie. On a professional level, I've been honored to connect with many incredible folks. I hear you, and I will continue to learn from you all: Dave Trottier, Carol Benanti, Chris Ramsey, Dr. J. (no need for any other explanation for such a superhero, right?), and Brett Pribble. So many more, such little space... Even if I missed your name, I appreciate you in my world and in my writing life. Thank you all. ~ Stella 2020

Acknowledgments

Dr. Charles Cooper

I would like to recognize Stella, who has made me better than I am during this process, Sheila Cooper, who has seen that Charles and Madelyn were fed and cared for while I was otherwise occupied, my father, who taught me to be everything I could be at everything I did all the time, finally, all the people who contributed to this book, their words, stories, thoughts, and ideas...

The thirty-three of you are the reason this book exists.

I wouldn't be a human being if I didn't say it gives me so much pride to publish the work of my son, Charles Cooper IV in this book. The Class of 2020 may never get to walk a stage; however, their lives will be so much more than ours ever were.